His Christmas Wish

TIA MARLEE

A NOVEL CHOICE

A NOVEL CHOICE PRESS

Book Cover by Sunset Rose Books

Editing by Lia Huntington

Proofread by Chrisandra's Corrections

Contents

To my mother who always said I should write a book. I only wish you were still here to see it come to fruition.

CHAPTER ONE

Morgan

OCTOBER

I GINGERLY CLOSE LIAM'S door, thankful he fell asleep easily tonight. Creeping down the hallway, I stop in the kitchen, grab the stack of unpaid bills from the island, and head to the worn table.

As I sink into the stiff wooden chair, I think, *I can do this.*

Dread sinks into my gut like a hot rock. I knew getting married before we finished college would mean struggling financially. What I didn't count on was losing William so soon, and all the bills that would come home in his place. The cost of burying the man I loved. The mortgage I have to cover alone. William and I talked about getting life insurance but put it off. We were young and had plenty of time.

Or so we thought.

Since he passed away two years ago, our savings has dwindled. Thankfully I'm able to take Liam to work with me. I can't imagine having to add daycare expenses to the running list of bills awaiting my attention.

I rub at my chest, willing away the ache that has taken up residence there. Tonight the sadness threatens to swallow me whole. It took a while for me to find my feet as a widowed mother. It's not easy, but some days I'm proud of how I've kept it together. Others, doubt creeps in. How am I supposed to raise Liam without the love of my life by my side?

Sometimes loneliness echoes in my soul, and I wonder if I am destined to be alone for the rest of my life. Will I ever love someone again? It's hard to think about opening my heart. I can't imagine meeting a man who would love Liam like his own. I'm not ready for anyone to try to take William's place.

Sighing, I open the first of the mail, sliding my finger under the sticky flap, and pulling the letter from inside. These days junk mail would be welcome. It seems no one sends letters anymore, only bills. I received some sympathy cards around the time of the funeral, but those dwindled to a stop leaving me alone in my sadness.

My pain is nothing compared to the broken heart of the five-year-old boy down the hall. For months Liam wouldn't sleep alone. Refusing his twin bed adorned with superhero blankets, he cuddled in with me, his chubby little hand tucked into mine.

Barely three when his father died, Liam didn't understand what was happening. Only that the dad who loved him wasn't coming home each day to tuck him in.

When we moved to Piney Brook, we were certain we could do it all alone. Our parents being halfway across the country didn't seem like a huge obstacle because we had each other. Especially when our parents were so determined to tear us apart. They thought we'd made a mistake getting married at only twenty years old. They wanted us to wait and were determined to make their opinions known every chance they got. Moving felt like a way for us to get out from under their negativity and start a life we could be proud of.

When William died, I considered moving back to Florida to be closer to our parents, but this is home. Liam was born here. We bought our first home here. I couldn't possibly leave William behind. It's important to me that Liam be close to his father.

I need to be close to him. Moving just isn't an option.

Tears start to make their way down my cheeks. Wiping furiously, I open another envelope. One by one I pay the bills I can, watching my bank balance sink lower and lower. Paydays come too far apart.

Who knew funerals were so expensive. William's parents paid some, but it still took a chunk of our savings. I wanted him to be comfortable, and they wanted him to have the best of everything.

I pour myself a glass of milk and head to the living room. Tucking my legs beneath me, I settle into the plush cushions of the couch and wrap myself in a soft blanket, a gift from our wedding. I hate going to bed and rolling over to William's side of the bed and meeting smooth sheets cold with his absence. I miss sleeping with him next to me, even if he did steal the covers.

I'm not ready for the cold bed, so I cuddle into the couch and flip on the TV. Mindless late night talk shows drown out my thoughts, and before long I'm nodding off.

A loud cry startles me awake. Flipping onto my side, I push myself up and bang my knee on the coffee table. Rubbing the throbbing knot with one hand, I half hop, half run to Liam's room just as he throws open the door sobbing. "Mommy," Liam gasps. "I had a bad dream."

I scoop him into my arms and hold him tight. "Shh, it's okay, bud," I whisper while rubbing comforting circles on his small back. "Mommy's here." Liam's cries begin to slow as I sway side to side with him in my arms as though he was still an infant. He's heavier now, but his sweet head on my shoulder is still the same. My baby boy.

As he starts to fall back asleep, I hold him close and creep down the hallway into my room.

Carefully lowering Liam onto William's side of the bed, I pause, staring at the little boy who shares so many of his dad's features. Soft brown curls top his head, and his cupid's bow lips turn down in a frown. The little freckle on his left cheek, the same as his dad's, peeks out from below his lash line.

I can't decide if fate is cruel for leaving behind a miniature William for me to raise alone, or kind for letting me see so much of him in our son.

Climbing under the sheets on my side of the bed, I scoot a bit closer to the sleeping boy beside me. Resting my hand on his little back, I breathe him in and hope for peaceful sleep.

"Mommy, Mommy! Get up! GET UP!" Liam shouts as he bounces on the bed. "Get *up*! I'm hungry!" Sliding off the side of the bed, he scampers down the hallway toward the kitchen. Saturday is pancake day, something William started when we moved into this house. A tradition I've kept up even when I couldn't bring myself to eat.

Slowly I push myself up to sit and put my feet on the floor. "I'm up, bud, I'll be there in a sec." Time and five-year-olds wait for no one. Sliding on my robe, I make my way down the hallway and meet Liam in the kitchen.

Standing proudly on the stool he must have dragged from the bathroom, he points to the mixing bowl and pancake mix he has put onto the kitchen island. "See, Mommy, I've got it all ready!" His eager eyes look up at me with all the hope and energy of a kid ready to face the weekend.

"You sure do." I pat his head and reach for the mix.

As Liam mixes, I heat the skillet and get down the plates. Everything in this kitchen reminds me of happier times. William and I loved to cook together. He said the kitchen is the heart of the home, and when we bought this house, that is just what he set out to create.

Kitschy little signs adorn the walls. A plaque proclaiming, "If I had to stir it, it's homemade"—my contribution to the kitchen decor—hangs centered between a large fork and spoon on the faded wallpapered walls.

Ladling the mix onto the griddle, I lean over and give Liam a kiss on the cheek. "What do you want to do this afternoon?"

"Can we go shopping for my Halloween costume?" His eyes sparkle with excitement. "You will never guess what I wanna be." A grin spreads across his face.

"Hmm, I bet you want to be a pickle," I guess.

Liam shakes his head, "Nuh uh, Mommy. Pickles are yucky." I chuckle. William didn't like pickles either. Like father, like son, I suppose.

"Okay, we will go see what your choices are, but I can't promise anything today. It might be a planning day." I see a bit of the shine leave his eyes and my heart cracks. It's hard to say no to my son.

After we finish breakfast and clean up, Liam and I head to the strip mall. I find a spot close to the front, and we pile out of the car, slipping coats over our long-sleeved shirts. The weather is still nice for fall, but there is a cool breeze today.

"Hold my hand while we're in the parking lot. I don't want you to get smooshed." I grab Liam's little hand, barely catching him before he sprints across the parking lot and into the Halloween store temporarily set up in the old grocery space.

Just inside the door is a huge, cackling, animatronic goblin. Liam takes one look and hides behind me, burying his head into the back of my legs. "It's all right, it isn't real, buddy. Let's go back there and find the costume you want."

It's early enough in the season that there aren't too many people shopping today. Liam runs right to the section of kids' costumes and starts digging through the overcrowded rack of brightly colored outfits. I don't see how anyone can find anything in the tangled mess of sleeves and hangers. It looks like Halloween exploded.

"Mommy! This one! This is what I want." He bounces from foot to foot grasping onto the sleeve of a costume hung haphazardly on the rack. I carefully pick up the costume he's clinging to for dear life—a bright red firefighter costume, complete with a spongy axe and black shoe covers.

"Oh my, Liam. You want to be a firefighter for Halloween?" I ask, smiling at his exuberance.

Nodding his little head and looking up at me, he says, "Please, Mommy, please, can we get it?"

Thinking about the bills last night, I look at the price tag. It's more than I had planned to spend, but I can't bring myself to say no. "Sure, buddy. Let's go pay." I'll just stretch the food budget a little further for the next two weeks. I can eat soup. It's getting cooler outside now anyway.

"YAY!" Liam grabs the costume from my hands and turns to run to the front.

"Walking feet, mister," I call.

"Yes, Mommy." Liam slows, but continues bouncing toward the registers, grinning with excitement.

My own step falters when I realize I'm smiling too. Genuinely smiling. Maybe I'm healing after all. We reach the checkout together, hand in hand. "I'm gonna be a fireman!" Liam says as he carefully hands over the costume. "I'm gonna help people when I grow up."

"That is wonderful. The world needs helpers," the cashier says kindly, her graying hair set into a neat bun atop her head. "What makes you want to be a fireman?"

"My daddy was sick, and my mommy said the firemans tried to help him. I want to help people too, and maybe they won't have to go away," Liam says sadly, a frown pulling at the edges of his lips.

"Oh," she says, her understanding eyes meet my gaze. "You're right. Firemen are heroes. I'm sure your daddy would be very proud of you."

The ache is back, sharp and hot. It's always the unexpected comments that are the hardest. I give a small nod of thanks as I try to keep the sadness at bay. Taking Liam's hand, we make our way to the car.

Opening the back door, I lay his costume on the seat and move to let him climb into his car seat. Making sure his straps are snug, I lean in and give his cheek a kiss. "I'm so glad you found what you wanted today," I say, taking a moment to breathe in his little-boy smell.

"Thank you, Mommy, I can't wait to wear it. Do you think I can wear it to school?"

I laugh as I get into the car and buckle myself. "Of course you can. On dress-up day."

Liam groans. "I want to wear it every day. Isn't that what real firemans do?"

"Well," I sigh. "They wear them at work, but they don't wear them all the time. Even real firemen wear regular clothes."

"Oh," Liam says. I know this conversation isn't over yet. He is one determined kid.

As I turn out of the parking lot, I ask, "Would you like to bake cookies when we get home?" Liam loves helping me cook, and I could use some sugar in my life right now.

The car starts to shake and pull to the right—the tell-tale wobble of a flat tire. Holding in a scream, I pull to the side of the road. "Looks like we have a flat tire. I'll need to figure out how to change it, okay? Stay put. I'll be right outside the car." He nods, happily holding onto the bag containing his costume.

"Okay, Mommy."

Popping the trunk, I make my way around the car to assess the damage. The front passenger-side tire is flat. Flatter than flat. Frustrated tears make their way to the surface, but I push them back. I've cried way too much the last few days, and I will not cry over a flat tire. It can't be too hard to change, right? People do this all the time.

I open the trunk, pull out the spare, and lean it against the side of the car, then go back and collect the jack and lug wrench. Kneeling, I stare at the jack. *How the heck does this thing work?*

I reach for my phone in my back pocket. Except, it's not there. It's probably still sitting on the table by the bills. Panic starts to settle in when it dawns on me that I can't call for help. Ugh, I messed up.

I get up, reach into the passenger side, and pop the glove box. As I'm flipping through the pages of the owner's manual, a black truck slows to a stop behind the car.

My nerves come roaring to life. Hopefully the man stepping out is here to help and not a serial killer who preys on stranded women.

"Ma'am, I see you are having some trouble. Flat tire?" The man's deep voice cuts into my panicked thoughts. Looking up, I'm face to face with a Chris Hemsworth look-alike. Dark brown hair—short on the sides, long on top—stands in all directions like he just ran his fingers through it. Gorgeous green eyes framed by thick black lashes, and a slight crook in his nose. Jeez, the man is gorgeous. I wonder what it would feel like to run my palm over the slight stubble covering his cheeks and chin.

"Ma'am?" he says again. "Can I help you change your tire?"

"Oh, oh. Yes, uhm, thank you. I'm sure you can see I have no idea what I am doing," I say with a nervous hitch. "Thanks, that would be great." Guilt rocks me. I can't believe I'm having such a strong reaction to someone I've never met before. How can I even think such things about someone other than William?

I pull at the hem of my shirt, smoothing it over my rounded hips. Losing your husband to an early heart attack is bad for the waistline.

"Mommy, can I get out now?" Liam yells from the back seat, breaking my stare. Thankful for the distraction, I lean into the car. "Why don't you stay put, that way you won't run around and get hurt."

Liam pouts. "But I want to watch the tire get changed."

Sighing, I open his door and unbuckle him. "Okay, but no running off—there are cars, and I don't want you to get hurt."

"Yes, Mommy," Liam says innocently. "I just want to watch."

The man chuckles. "It's all right, he can be my helper. My name is Brant, by the way. I own Brant's Auto Shop down the road."

"See, Mom! I can be a helper!" Liam squirms in my arms until I sit him down. "I'm Liam, and that's my mommy. I'm going to be a fireman one day and be a helper too. Are you a fireman in regalar clothes?"

Brant laughs, sticking out his hand to Liam for a shake. "No, I'm not a fireman, I'm a mechanic. That means I work on cars."

Liam studies Brant's every move as he makes short work of loosening the lug nuts and jacking up the car. "Liam, can you be a big helper and hold these when I take them off? If they fall in the grass they'll be hard to find."

Liam nods sagely, taking this responsibility seriously. He sticks out his little hands and waits patiently as Brant drops the lug nuts into his palms. In no time Brant has the old tire off and the spare on. He heads back to his truck and comes back with some wet wipes. He hands one to Liam. "Better clean up. Don't want to get anything on your clothes."

Liam diligently wipes his hands, and then holds them up to me to see. "Did I get it all, Mommy?"

Brant finishes wiping his own hands and passes me a card. "You'll need to have that tire replaced. The nail went in pretty close to the sidewall, and a spare isn't meant to be driven on for the long haul. You can come in anytime and I'll help you out with that if you want."

I panic. I don't have money for a new tire right now. I barely have money for groceries, and bills are still piling up. "Can it wait two weeks if I don't go very far, do you think?" I ask, shame lacing my words and causing heat to fill my cheeks.

"Well," Brant says, looking over at Liam who is focused on our conversation. "Not really. It's a temporary fix. Why don't you come in now, and I'll see if I've got a replacement on hand?"

I hesitate. I really don't have the money for this right now. "I'm sorry," I say, embarrassment causing my cheeks to heat. "It will have to wait, I just don't have the funds at the moment. Plus, I can't miss work." If my pants ripped down the middle right now I couldn't be more humiliated. Admitting to a complete stranger that my finances are a mess is not my idea of a fun Saturday afternoon.

"We are gonna make cookies. Do you like cookies?" Liam asks. "We can make you cookies, and you can fix our tire. Deal?" He sticks out his hand like he has negotiated things like this a million times.

"Liam, this isn't something we can trade for cookies. Tires are expensive," I say softly. "I'm so sorry, they are learning about bartering in school right now," I stammer. Could the ground just swallow me whole, please?

"I love cookies actually. What kind are you making? If you say chocolate chip, you've got yourself a deal," Brant says, reaching out and shaking Liam's hand.

"I couldn't possibly let you replace my tire for cookies. I can pay you back when I get paid. I just don't have the money today," I say, exasperated. No one wants to work for free, and this man has a business to run.

"Seriously, don't worry about it. I own the shop—if I want to help someone out, I do. And, your son drives a hard bargain, Ms..." Brant draws out the last part of the sentence and I realize I still haven't given him my name.

"You can call me Morgan. I really appreciate this. You have no idea," I say, reaching out to shake his hand. When our palms connect a tingle shoots up my arm causing me to yank my hand back too quickly. "I'm sorry, I— That was rude," I slide my hand down my leg trying to rid myself of that tingly feeling. I haven't reacted to a man like that since the day I met William.

"It's all right, I get it. I'm always honored to lend a hand when it's in my wheelhouse. Follow me to my shop and I'll take a look." Brant turns to walk to his truck. "Who knows, I may have a used tire in the back I can throw on to get you through," he calls over his shoulder, then hops into his big truck without waiting for me to respond.

"Back into your seat, bud. Looks like we have one more stop to make. I hope you're ready to bake a lot of cookies."

Liam scrambles back into his seat. "I can help, Mommy. I'm a good helper."

"That you are, little man. That you are," I say, sliding into my seat and starting the car. I take a deep breath and cross my fingers that there is a used tire that will work and buy me more time. Otherwise, we'll be bartering cookies for rides to work.

CHAPTER TWO

Brant

I HAVE NO IDEA what just happened. One minute I'm helping the blonde-haired curvy goddess change a tire, and the next I am tingling head to toe from a handshake. Shaking my head, I climb into my truck and wait for her to be ready to go. Seeing her move around to her side of the car and close the door, I wait a second before I motion for her to follow. I pull out and make my way back to the shop, making sure she stays right behind me.

My mind wanders back to Morgan standing on the side of the road looking lost, her blonde hair dancing in the breeze. She looked so small standing there flipping through the owner's manual.

Stopping was a no brainer—I would have stopped for anyone—but after that handshake, I find myself wondering if she's single. I didn't notice a ring, but that doesn't mean she isn't taken. I turn into the shop parking lot and motion for her to pull in front of one of the bay doors.

I park and head inside to open the door for her car. Flipping on the lights in the shop always brings me a sense of pride. The two-bay shop may be small, but it's mine. Rolling up the outside door, I inhale the mix of fresh fall air and oil. *Home.*

Morgan and Liam are waiting beside her car. "C'mon, I'll show you where you can hang out while I work." I gesture for them to follow me into the small waiting room just off the side of the first bay. "Watch your step, the floor might be slippery." Morgan holds onto Liam like she is afraid he will slide into the next town, but the little guy manages just fine. "You can wait in here. There's a TV in the corner and usually a kids' movie in the DVD player. I'll come get you when I'm done."

Morgan gives a small smile, but Liam is already squirming in place. "I don't want to watch a movie. Can I be your helper again?" His hopeful face is too cute to turn down.

"If it's okay with your mom, and you promise to follow directions, you can sit on a stool while I work." I pause and look to Morgan for her approval. "Watching is like helping because you are learning how to help when you're bigger."

"Are you sure?" she asks, giving Liam what might look like a smile if she wasn't grimacing. "He can be a handful and has a hard time being still sometimes."

"I'm sure. My buddy brings his daughter in all the time. We have a chair Elli sits on where she is plenty away from the action, but it's totally up to you." Liam looks ready to combust trying to be still while he waits on his mom to decide—and I'm feeling some of that, too.

"Okay," she hesitates. "Liam, sit still and listen. If you give Mr. Brant too much trouble, you'll be right back in here with me."

"Yes, Mama," Liam yells as he takes off for the door.

"Whoa, slow down, champ," I say, grabbing hold of his hand. "Remember, I said it's slippery out here. We can't have you getting hurt, now can we? Why don't you stay here with your mama while I pull the car inside, then I'll come get you."

Liam nods. "Last time I got hurted, mommy cried." His excitement seems to fade a bit with the memory.

"Moms worry about us. That's their job," I say, shooting a wink at Morgan. Liam tilts his head to the side like he is considering what I said. Laughing, I ruffle his hair on my way out to the shop.

Once the car is in place, I grab Liam from the waiting room. "There you go, bud, sit on that chair right there."

"Okay!" Liam bounces excitedly on the chair, but he doesn't get down. "Liam, do you have toy cars at home?" I ask. "I loved cars when I was your age."

Liam's smile stretches across his face. "I have some cars at home, but I really want a big racetrack that I can play with." He swings his legs back and forth, causing the chair to squeak a little. "I'm gonna ask Santa."

"How fun! I loved those when I was your age." Pulling the flat tire from the trunk, I confirm the nail is too close to the sidewall for a quick patch. "All right," I say, sighing. "Let's go see if it's our lucky day and there is a used tire we can put on here for your mom."

Liam slides off the chair and takes my hand. "You can keep me company while I look," I say, giving his hand a little squeeze. We make our way to the back of the shop where we keep the used tires. Liam helps me inspect some I pull down from the stack, but none are in good enough condition that I want to put them on their car.

We make our way back to the waiting room where Morgan is flipping through a magazine I picked up recently. *Better Homes and Gardens.* One of our female customers said we needed something besides car magazines. Guess she was right. I make a mental note to grab a bigger selection next time I'm at the store.

Morgan looks up as we enter, and smiles. "Done already? That was fast." Getting a look at my face, her smile falls. "Oh, so *not* done, then."

Her deflated tone makes my stomach twitch. "Well, unfortunately, I was right, and the nail is too close to the sidewall to repair, which means you'll need a whole new tire. We checked out back, but the used tires I have in that size are no good. I don't keep new tires on hand here, so I'll have to get you one on Monday. And actually, all four tires look like they need to be replaced. The tread is pretty low."

"How much time do I have? With the holidays coming up, I was trying to hold off on any major repairs until the new year." If she keeps wringing her hands together like that, she is going to rub the skin raw. I don't like seeing her upset, but I shake it off. She's a grown woman—I'm sure she can handle herself. Customers want to put off repairs all the time, but it's my job to let them know what they need.

"I think you have a little bit of time, but until the new year is probably pushing it. I can set you up with a line of credit through the shop if you want. You can pay me back a little at a time. It's not safe to drive on tires with low tread, especially with winter coming, and precious cargo."

It's not completely unheard of for me to offer a line of credit for something small, but a set of tires is a little more than I'd usually cover. It came out before I knew what I was saying. After a beat, I realize I don't regret it. I'd rather eat the cost if she disappears than have something happen to her and Liam.

"Oh, do you have a company you work with to do financing?" she asks, perking up.

"Uh, no. Not really," I say slowly. "It would be a personal loan of sorts."

She is already shaking her head no before I finish my thought. "No way, I can't accept that, and it goes far beyond a payment of cookies. That is a lot of money. I'll have to figure something else out." Her mind seems made up, but she looks as though the weight of the world is on her shoulders. I can't let her leave like that.

"Morgan, really, I don't mind. How about you cook me dinner once a week as payment? I'll trust you to set the cost of the dinners. It's a win-win really, I won't be eating microwave dinners, and you'll be able to drive around safely."

She pauses a minute, refusal written all over her face.

"Let him be a helper, Mommy. You said helpers are 'portant," Liam chimes in, pulling on her hand.

Morgan frowns and I can hear the wheels turning in her head.

"I guess that might work. I can cook you dinner on Wednesdays if you're free. It's early-release day at school, so I'll have time to prepare. I'm still paying back every penny, though!" She looks resigned, and pink colors her cheeks. Is she embarrassed to have to accept my help, or did she feel that same pull of attraction when we touched on the side of the road?

"I don't have to eat at your place. I know your significant other would be uncomfortable with that. You can drop something off here." I'm holding my breath hoping she invites me to have dinner with them. She fascinates me, and the feeling I got when we shook hands still ghosts on my skin.

"No, no. It's fine. No significant other, so no worries there. You can come over and eat with us. Less work for me that way, and you've been so kind." She smiles. "Is it safe enough to drive home tonight?"

"Yeah, but I'd feel better if I could follow you home. Just in case something happens. That spare isn't in the best shape either." It'd do her no good to get stuck on the side of the road again—at least not without me there.

"Uhm, okay. I guess that's fine," she says with a sigh. "I appreciate it, but you're going so far out of your way for us, and I can't figure out why." She eyes me curiously.

I shrug. I'm not entirely sure why either. "I own my own business. I've worked hard to get where I am. If I want to help someone occasionally, I can," I say. "I'll pull your car back out and then we'll close up."

I pull her car out into the gravel lot before heading back in to close the bay door and flip off all the lights. I relock the building and prepare to leave. Morgan and Liam are already settled in her car, so I head over and lean down to the open window. "I'll follow you home. Once you're inside, I'll head on." Tapping the top of the car, I turn and stride to my truck.

Driving behind her, my mind goes to Liam and his hope for a big racetrack for Christmas. Every little boy should have a racetrack, but Morgan seems so worried about her finances...

Giving myself a mental kick, I slow as she pulls into a gravel driveway leading up to a cute one-story cottage-looking house. The yellow paint has started to fade, and the trees dotting the front yard could use a trim, but it's a homey place.

I wait until they are on the front porch, and Morgan has the door open before I roll my window down to say goodbye.

"Wait a sec, please," Morgan calls. She leans down and says something to Liam who waves and scampers into the house. She turns and heads to the passenger side of the truck. "I appreciate all of your help today. I can drop my car off on Monday, if that works for you. I'll have a friend pick us up."

"Sure." I nod. "That works. I wrote down what size tires you need, so I'll grab them on my way in to work on Monday. Drive carefully, though. Stay off the highway, and don't go far on that donut of a spare."

Catching her eyes with mine I spot golden flecks in the brown of her eyes. I hadn't noticed that earlier. Coupled with her thick wavy blonde hair, and fair skin, she is really, breathtakingly beautiful.

Realizing I'm staring like a creeper, I clear my throat. "Well, okay. See you Monday, then. Oh, and tell Liam I hope he has fun baking those cookies."

A smile lights her face. "Thanks. Yeah, great. I forgot about the cookies. I'll make sure we bring some on Monday, too." Her cheeks blush a pretty shade of pink. "I… well. Thanks again," she mumbles, stepping back from the truck.

"No problem," I say, and put the truck in gear. "See ya." I pull away as she stands for another minute staring at the truck like she is trying to figure me out. *Good luck, Morgan. I have no idea what is happening either.*

Chapter Three

Morgan

Sighing, I wrap my arms around my middle as I watch Brant drive away. My very own modern-day fairy tale hero. I admit, when he got out of his truck on the side of the road I was intimidated—six feet tall, dark hair, green eyes, a broad chest, and strong arms. He looked like he belonged in a magazine, not on the side of the road changing my tire.

He was so kind and patient with Liam. I just hope he means it when he says I can pay him back over time. Shame burns through my gut at the idea of owing someone, but the need to keep Liam safe trumps any negativity I might feel. I'll just have to offer to work after-school care to make up the difference.

Resigned, I turn and make my way back to the house.

"Mommy! I got all the stuff for the cookies out. Mr. Brant said chocolate chips are his favorite." Liam drags me into the kitchen. The island counter is covered with ingredients. "Can we bake cookies now? We have to make lots so Mr. Brant can have some too."

"Sure," I say, grabbing the bowl. "Why don't you grab your stool and wash your hands?" I watch as Liam races out of the room. I wish I had his energy. Making sure he gathered everything we need, I set up while I wait for him to come back.

The smell of chocolate chip cookies baking fills the house and dozens of cookies line the counters. I love baking. It's comforting, and the smell always lingers, making it feel like home. "Liam, why don't you help me make a plate for Mr. Brant?" I ask, grabbing down a platter. "That way they will be extra special when we give them to him on Monday."

Liam takes his time picking the best ones and layering them on the plate. "Do you think he will like them?" The hopeful note in his voice reminds me that he struck the bargain to begin with.

"Of course he will. I've never met anyone who doesn't like getting their favorite cookie as payment. Have you?" I ask, smiling.

"No, I love when you give me cookies!" Liam smiles content-edly down at the platter. "I think it's ready."

Monday morning comes way too fast these days. I wish there was a day between Sunday and the start of the week. Making my way down the hallway to the kitchen, I pop my head into Liam's room. He's kicked the covers off, one leg hangs off the side of the bed, and his favorite stuffed dinosaur is clutched in his little hand.

"Liam, time to get up for school, buddy."

Liam groans and rolls over, pulling his blankets over his head. He's not a morning person either. At least he got *that* from me, I guess.

Popping a coffee pod into the machine, I press start and move to the pantry. Morning breakfast is usually toast or cereal, but today is a little cool. Grabbing some oatmeal packets, I turn to find Liam standing in the middle of the kitchen, little pieces of hair sticking up everywhere, and his misbuttoned pajama top twisted to the side. Seeing the oatmeal in my hand he gives a little nod and yawns. "I'm tired, Mommy. Why does school start so early?" His little voice hoarse with sleep. Liam takes a seat at the table, and I place his oatmeal in front of him.

It's a bit earlier than usual today since we have to drop the car off to Brant. Thank goodness Susan agreed to meet us there and drive us to school. It pays to work with your best friend.

"Go brush your teeth and get dressed—we leave soon."

Liam stands, taking his empty bowl to the sink.

"Don't forget to brush your hair too." I pat the top of his head as he walks by.

"Yes, Mommy," Liam says, dragging his feet as he slumps down the hallway to his room. Satisfied he is getting ready, I head down the hall to get myself ready for the day. Forty minutes later, cookies in tow, we are pulling into the parking lot of Brant's Auto Shop. His truck is parked alongside the building, and the bay doors are already open.

The building is small, but clean. Dark blue paint covers the outside walls, with the name painted in white across the front. It looks professional and tidy. The sound of air tools and music hint that the shop has been open for a while now. Seeing that Susan isn't here yet, I let out a sigh of relief. We made it on time.

I unbuckle Liam's seat and grab my bag. Handing him the plate of cookies, I spot Brant coming out of his shop.

"Good morning." His rich voice carries across the parking lot. "What do you have there?" he asks Liam.

Liam beams. "We made you cookies, just like I said." He hands the platter to Brant. "Chocolate chip, a'cuz those are your favorites."

Brant smiles, taking the platter and lifting the plastic wrap a bit on the side. Putting his face to the plate, he inhales. "They smell delicious. Did you help?"

Liam starts bouncing in place. "I did. Mom let me mix the 'gredients and I helped spoon them onto the tray to bake." He points to the plate. "I picked all the best ones for you a'cuz you helped my mommy."

Brant looks a bit surprised by Liam's declaration but recovers quickly and smiles. "Thanks, bud. I bet they will taste great after I eat my lunch." He winks at Liam and gestures with the tray in the direction of the door. "Let's get these inside so we don't make your mom late."

Liam reaches for Brant's hand as they walk toward the front door. Brant pauses a minute, and then takes Liam's little hand in his. The gesture is so sweet, it makes my chest ache. And not in the way I'm used to.

Weird.

Following them inside the entrance, I pass a long countertop with a computer and chair behind it. Old car posters line the wood paneled walls. In the middle of them sits a framed photo of Brant and a beautiful older woman. Brant's gaze goes to the photo.

"My mom and I when I first opened this place. She was so proud." There is a sadness in his voice. "She passed away a year ago now. She was my hero." Clearing his voice, he sets the cookies on the counter as he walks behind it and grabs a sticker to put on my keychain.

"You're all set, Morgan," he says, handing me a slip of paper. "This has my personal number, and the number of the shop on it. Call me when you're done at work. I can run your car up to you."

Taking the paper, I slip it inside my bag. "Oh, you don't have to do that. Susan said she could bring us back by. I have the spare booster seat with me, so it won't be a problem."

Brant looks at me intently for a moment. I shiver a bit, feeling almost like he can see through me.

"No problem. If that changes, just let me know." He shoots me a half smile and looks through the front window. "It looks like your friend may have just gotten here. Do you need help getting anything out of the car?"

"Nope, I just need to grab the extra seat and I'm all set," I say. "C'mon, Liam, Mrs. Susan is here to take us to school."

"Hey," Susan says as we come out. "Sorry I'm a few minutes late. Monday, you know." She comes around to the passenger side and opens the rear door.

"No problem," I tell her, loading Liam's seat into the car. "We just got here a couple of minutes ago too." Motioning for Liam to hop up in the booster, I reach my bag over and drop it into the front passenger seat.

"Whoa," Susan says under her breath. "Who is that fine looking man?"

I glance back through the shop window where Brant is straightening the magazines in the waiting area. "*That* is Brant," I say in a stage whisper. "Stop staring at him. It's rude." Shaking my head, I close Liam's door. "Besides, you're happily married, remember?"

She gives me a look that implies I've lost my mind. "I'm married, not blind," she says, laughing. She stops when she notices I'm not laughing along. "What's wrong, Morgan? Did he say something to you?"

"I've agreed to make him dinner once a week until I can pay back the cost of the tires. This whole ordeal is way out of my budget." The words spill out of my mouth. I am freaking out and really need someone to talk to about all of this. Since William died, Susan is my person.

Her mouth drops open in shock. "You agreed to make him dinner? Every week? What has gotten into you? You never let a man around Liam."

"He isn't a man. I mean, he is, obviously. I'm not dating him though. He was nice enough to help me and has gone out of his way to do so. Making an extra helping of dinner is the least I can do, honestly." I point to Liam in the backseat who has already nodded off. "Plus, Liam seems to look up to him. He's talked about him nonstop since we got home on Saturday."

Avoiding her intense stare, I turn and climb into the car, effectively ending the conversation. After a minute, the driver's side door opens and Susan slides in. "You like him." She says it like it's a fact. "I'll be darned."

Shaking my head, I gape at her. "No! It's not like that. He is helping me out, I'm helping him have a meal instead of take out. That is it. Nothing more. I'm not ready to date again. I might never be ready." The words sound more determined in my head but come out with a hint of question.

"You like him. It's okay to like someone again, hun. It's been two years." Susan reaches over and gives my hand a little squeeze and starts the car. The rest of the ride to school is quiet leaving me to stew in my own thoughts.

That afternoon, I'm packing my bag when Susan comes strolling in. "Ready to go get your car from hot stuff?" She grins. "I know I am ready to take another look. Maybe he has an employee I can invite over for dinner." She waggles her eyebrows suggestively.

"Stop it." I laugh. "You know darn well Sam would be upset to find another man in his dinner spot."

"Well, a woman can dream," she says with a giggle. "Sam and I have been married so long, I doubt he would even bat an eyelash. He knows he has nothing to worry about."

I shake my head. "You two are adorable, and you are a mess."

"Yes, but I'm a fun mess. Like confetti, here to brighten your day." She winks. "Let's grab Liam and get going."

A few minutes later we are in her car on the way to Brant's. I gave him a call after classes ended, and he said my car was ready to go. Thank goodness. I can't stand not being able to drive myself. Pulling into the parking lot, I see my car parked in one of the guest spots. It's suspiciously cleaner than when I dropped it off.

"Thanks again for the ride, Susan. I owe you one," I say stepping out of the car, throwing my bag over my shoulder. Susan hops out and helps Liam from the car.

"Well, get Hottie McHottie's number in there and we'll call it even. You need a night on the town." Susan laughs at herself while I shake my head at her. I don't dare tell her he already gave it to me this morning. She would never let it go.

Closing the door, I laugh and make my way to where Liam and Susan now stand in front of the car. The shop is busy. Both bay doors are open, and several cars line the front of the gravel parking lot.

"Stay with me, Liam. Don't go running around. There are too many cars. You'll get hurt." Taking Liam by the hand, I say goodbye to Susan, and we make our way to the waiting room door.

There are several cars parked on the side of the building where the parking lot loops around. Brant's truck is parked in the same spot it was this morning. Nerves light under my skin at the thought of seeing him again. Hurrying my step, we make it to the door just as it swings open.

"Morgan, I was starting to wonder if you were gonna show." Brant smiles. "I'm just kidding." He reaches out and touches my arm lightly for half a second, taking my breath away. "I'm glad you're here. Let me grab your keys and we can give her a test drive." He pops behind the counter for the keys before I register what's happening. Can someone really be stunned stupid by a handsome guy?

Shaking my head, I clear my throat and wipe my hands on my jeans. "No need. I'm sure you've done that. I'll just pay you what I can and get out of your hair." *Is my voice always this squeaky?* Flames lick up my neck and race toward my cheeks. I'm sure I'm fire engine red—darn my fair skin.

"Oh, all right then." Brant comes around the counter holding my keys. "If you're sure." He looks at me, and then to the floor like he's trying to gather his thoughts. He's disappointed? Straightening his shoulders, he smiles. "Listen, Morgan—about the dinners. You really don't have to do that. I'm fine with you paying me back when you can."

My head shakes so hard, pieces of hair start to slip from my ponytail. "Absolutely not. No way. A deal is a deal. Plus, I think Liam is excited to have a man to talk cars with." Liam squeezes my hand.

"Did you like the cookies we made for you?" Liam asks.

"They were so good I decided to share," Brant says, patting his stomach. "My guys said they were the best cookies they've ever had." He winks at me and I feel my cheeks flush. Liam's face lights up, a huge smile plastered across his face. He certainly looks pleased to have Brant's approval.

It kills me that Liam has no positive male role models in his life. William's old friends tried to step in after his heart attack, but they petered out after a while. I can't say I blame them. I was closed off and refused to allow anyone to help. I'd never felt so out of control and being in charge helped me stay sane.

"If you're sure. I don't want to intrude, but I certainly don't want to let Liam down," Brant says, bringing the conversation back around to the dinners. "He's a cute kid. Tough negotiator too. Does he get that from his dad, or from you?" Brant's handsome face tilts to the side a bit like he's trying to figure me out.

"He probably got it from his dad. I've never been good at negotiating. William was the one who handled anything like that." I smile sadly, bringing my hand to my chest expecting the ache that usually accompanies talking about him.

Startled that it doesn't come, I drop my hand to my side. The sharp feeling isn't there. I just feel a soft sort of sadness. I decide it's better to share the whole thing now. Like ripping a bandaid off—quick, so it only hurts for a second. "He died a little over two years ago. He had a heart attack at work."

Brant looks away quickly, drawing his hand over his short, trimmed beard. "I'm sorry, Morgan. I didn't realize... I—I'm sorry." He looks back to me, compassion making the fine lines at his eyes a little deeper. "I don't know what to say."

"That's okay," I say, and I realize it's true. "It's a tough situation, but we are getting through." I squeeze Liam's little hand and hold out the other for my keys. "Anyway, I just thought I should tell you before you come over on Wednesday. Sometimes Liam wants to talk about his dad, and other times he doesn't."

Brant drops the keys into my hand and reaches behind me to open the door. "Completely understandable," he says smiling softly at Liam. "It's hard to talk about my mom sometimes too." Standing back, he motions for me to move through the door first.

Jogging ahead of me a bit, he reaches out and opens the car door. "She's all set—new tires, new belts, and a bath. You should be good to go for a while."

My mouth drops open and I feel my chest flush with frustration. "New tires *and* new belts?" My hands clench at my sides. I know it is silly to be so upset. Brant is only helping me, and while I appreciate it, I don't like being indebted to anyone. "We agreed on tires. I didn't know you were doing anything else."

"Your belts were dry and cracked. It was a matter of time before they broke. It's fine, Morgan, belts are cheap. On the house." His eyes rake over the car. "I couldn't let you leave with new tires and bad belts."

"Anything else I should know about?" I ask, my tone clipped. How am I going to pay for new tires, belts, and Christmas in a few months. Liam desperately wants a racetrack and those are pricey. Anxiety slides down my throat like broken glass.

Brant looks uncertain and hesitates, taking in the look on my face. He grimaces slightly before hiding his expression. "Nope." Something about his one-word response raises the hair on the back of my neck. He's hiding something.

"Fine, don't tell me, but I'm going to find out one way or another. It's going to take me forever to pay you back at this rate." I huff, throwing my bag across to the passenger seat. "Thank you—I know you're only trying to help. I'm just a bit overwhelmed at the moment," I say, sliding into the car. I know what I said is true, but it still stings. "Do you have any allergies I should know about?"

"Allergies?" Brant looks confused for a minute. "Oh, for dinner. Uhm, no, no allergies. I don't like mushrooms though." The corner of his very kissable mouth lifts slightly. "So, I'll see you Wednesday, then?"

Nodding my head, I start the car. "Plan for six—is that okay? Liam needs to be in bed by eight or he's a bear to wake up in the morning."

"Six is fine. I'll see you then, Morgan. Thank you." I nod, clicking my seat belt into place as he closes my door and backs away. "See ya later, little man," he calls, waving at Liam.

Taking a deep breath, I head for home. I need some time to process all of this before I see him again in two days. Hopefully by then I will have a grip on my emotions.

CHAPTER FOUR

Brant

I STAND IN THE gravel parking lot watching Morgan's taillights fade for far too long. I know she doesn't feel entirely comfortable about our arrangement, but I'm glad she didn't take me up on my offer to avoid dinners. I'm looking forward to spending more time with her, and with Liam.

She would be so mad at me if she knew just how much I had done to her car. Tires and belts weren't the only things that needed fixing. I'd given the car a complete once-over, noting everything that needed repair and Daniel, my assistant, and closest thing to family I have left, worked like crazy with me to get it all done today. Oil change, fluids checked, new battery, new belts, new tires, new spark plugs .. Her car should be good to go for a while at least.

Daniel walks out of the shop, a rag in his hand. "She take the news okay?"

"I didn't even tell her about most of it," I say shaking my head. "She already felt anxious about letting me help her with the tires. If I told her about everything else, she would have flipped, I'm sure."

Daniel looks at me, his eyebrows drawn in like he is thinking of how to say what's on his mind.

"What's up, D? Don't hold back now," I say laughing. Daniel is nothing if not honest. Sometimes to a fault, but it's why we get along so well.

"I'm just wondering. What made you want to do all that for her?" He looks truly puzzled. Join the club buddy.

"I have no idea." I sigh and put my hands in my pockets. "Would you believe me if I told you I just didn't want her kid to be in an unsafe car?"

Daniel laughs and shakes his head. "Not a chance." Thankfully, he doesn't say anything else, and heads back into the shop. We still have a few hours left, and thanks to me hogging Daniel all day, Evan, the other technician that works for me, has gotten behind on our scheduled work. Looks like I'll be rolling up my sleeves and helping out. At least it will keep me from trying to find answers I'm not sure I'm ready for.

Wednesday afternoon, I leave the shop early to take a shower and get ready for dinner. Daniel and Evan didn't give me too much crap, thankfully. Daniel even encouraged me to "knock her socks off." Looking at the seat beside me, I hope I didn't overstep. I question myself for the thousandth time.

I shake my head. It's too late now. Grabbing the flowers and juice boxes, I take a deep breath and get out of the truck. Liam bounds down the front porch steps and excitedly runs towards me. "Mr. Brant, you're here! I like your truck, it's big!" He's grinning. "Mommy made meatloaf and 'tatoes and baby trees."

He grabs at my free hand and practically drags me inside. "Do you like baby trees?" His face is screwed up into a look of disgust. "I don't like baby trees, but Mommy said I need to eat them and grow big and strong if I wanna be a fireman one day."

"I'm sure your mom is right," I say bewildered. *What the heck are baby trees?* I'm guessing it's broccoli, but why wouldn't she just call it that?

Stepping into Morgan's house is like stepping into my childhood home. A comfy sofa sits against the back wall. An overstuffed armchair sits nearby in the same shade of beige. Throw pillows announcing "It's Fall Y'all" and "Pumpkin Patch" take up space on the cushions. Large windows make the space feel bigger than it actually is.

Pictures of Liam at different ages are hung on the wall behind the sofa. A picture of a younger Morgan and a handsome dark-haired man hung in the center. She was a beautiful bride.

"You made it." Morgan's soft voice pulls my attention back to her and Liam. Her surprised look makes me nervous again. Was she hoping I wouldn't come?

Holding out the bouquet of mixed flowers, my hand shakes slightly. "I saw these and thought you might like them." She takes the flowers and pulls them to her face, breathing in their soft scent. A bit of pink colors her cheeks and my heart races.

"I brought these for you, bud. Do you like apple juice?" I ask, passing the boxes off to Liam.

"I love apple juice!" Liam takes off through the entryway to the kitchen, juice boxes in hand.

"What do you say to Mr. Brant, Liam?" Morgan shouts after him.

"Thank you, Mr. Brant," he calls from the other room.

"Thank you, you didn't have to do that," Morgan says, avoiding my eyes.

It feels like I made her uncomfortable. Dang it. I just wanted to make her smile. "I'm sorry if it's too much. I just thought you were making me dinner, and my momma taught me you never show up empty handed." Leaning down, I take off my boots and set them by the door.

She looks even more beautiful tonight than I've ever seen her. Her blonde hair in loose waves down past her shoulders. She is in baggy jeans and a soft pink sweater, her feet bare. Pink polish peeks out from the hem of her jeans.

"You look beautiful." My cheeks warm at the comment. I didn't mean to say that out loud. She already looks spooked.

"Thank you." She blushes. "Follow me, dinner is almost done, and I should put these in water." She turns to walk into the same room Liam had disappeared to.

"Wait," I say, stopping her. "What are baby trees?" I ask her quietly.

She starts laughing and spins around to face me. "Oh my gosh." She giggles. "It's broccoli. Liam doesn't like it, but I told him they are baby trees that help him grow big and strong. I hope you like meatloaf." Still laughing, she makes her way into the kitchen.

I'm still standing in the same spot, my feet rooted to the floor. She is always stunning, but when she laughs, she is radiant—like the weight of the world isn't on her shoulders. I vow right then to make her laugh again.

When I walk into the kitchen, Liam is sitting at the small dinner table, and already has a juice box open, the little straw poking out the top. To the right, an island countertop is covered with a tray of meatloaf, a bowl of mashed potatoes, a gravy boat, a bowl of broccoli, and a platter of rolls. It smells delicious.

"You didn't have to go to all this trouble," I say at the same time my stomach lets out a loud grumble. "It smells amazing. Meatloaf is one of my favorite meals."

Smiling, she hands me a plate and grabs a smaller plate with little dividers on it for Liam. I stand back, giving her time to make his plate. "Wait for us," she says to Liam, setting the little blue plate in front of him. He nods and puts his hands under his thighs for good measure.

Chuckling, I hand her a plate. "Ladies first." She shakes her head like she is about to disagree with me. "My momma would have my hide if I didn't let you plate your food first."

She closes her mouth and smiles. "Guess I can't argue with that." She fills her plate and makes her way to sit by Liam who is squirming in his seat. I take my fill of the food and join them at the table. Poor Liam looks like he might just dive in head first if we don't eat soon.

"Let's eat." Liam grabs his fork and dives into his mashed potatoes. He shovels the food into his mouth faster than he can chew and swallow. "Slow down, Liam! You're going to choke." Morgan laughs.

He pauses and swallows the food currently puffing his little cheeks out like a chipmunk. "Sorry, Mommy, I'm just real hungry." He takes a smaller bite and looks at her. Nodding, she smiles back at him.

"Sorry, we usually use better table manners than this." She shakes her head with a small smile.

"I can't say I blame him," I say, moaning as the meatloaf hits my tongue. It's one of my favorites, but not many people make it right. "This is the best meatloaf I've ever had." I'm not kidding either. The flavor is perfect—just the right blend of spices, and the meat is moist. I don't know what sauce she used, but it is a bit sweet and tangy at the same time. "What did you put on the top?"

"I can't tell you that," she says with a small smile. "Chef's secret."

The rest of the meal passes fairly quietly. Everyone is focused on their food, and Liam sips at the juice box with a smile on his face.

Everyone finishes, and the plates get stacked on the counter. I lean over the sink and roll up my sleeves. "I'll get those later," Morgan says from behind me.

"No, ma'am—you cook, I clean. It's fair." Turning on the water, I get started on the dishes. Her little kitchen doesn't have a dishwasher, and no way am I leaving her to clean all this up after she was nice enough to make me dinner. I know she is doing it to ease her guilt and soothe her pride, but she doesn't need another thing to worry about.

"Suit yourself," she says, opening a cupboard and pulling out some plastic storage containers. "Would you like some of this to take home? Liam and I won't eat it all."

"Sure, I'd love some. I can bring your dishes back next week if that works."

This feels so nice. Being in the kitchen, cleaning up after a home-cooked meal. I was so busy establishing my business, I didn't have time to date. Now I am approaching my mid-thirties, and things just don't work out as easy at this age. Most women my age are married, and younger women don't seem to have the same goals in life I do.

I always wanted this. Domestic bliss. Growing up with just my mom, I missed the idea of a dad. My mom did her best, but there were things I didn't feel comfortable talking about with her. Especially as I got older. There are some things a boy just needs his dad for.

"Here, let me dry." Morgan steps beside me with a hand towel and reaches for the dishes dripping in the drainer.

I glance to my side and take in her profile. She really is lovely. Her arm brushes mine as she reaches for another dish, and those same sparks from the handshake light my flesh. My eyes search her for any sign she feels it too.

A small blush creeps up her neck, and her breath hitches just a bit. Almost imperceptible, but I caught it. Taking a breath, I turn and catch her eyes with mine. "Morgan, I..." I sigh. "Thank you for dinner." Something about the nervousness in her eyes makes me pause. She may feel it, but she isn't ready to explore whatever this is.

"I'll go ahead and get out of your hair. I'm sure you need to get Liam ready for bed." I roll my sleeves back down and pick up the to-go bag she set on the counter island. "Thanks again for dinner."

I walk into the small living room and see Liam playing on the soft beige and brown rug, cars strewn about him everywhere. "Hey bud, nice collection." He jumps up, a faded red car in his hands, and rushes towards me.

"Thanks! These were my daddy's when he was little." He grins. "This is my favorite. It's red and goes fast."

Taking the car, I examine it slowly. "Very nice," I say, handing it back. "This is an excellent choice. A Camaro. I always wanted one of these when I was your age."

Liam nods, "It's a'cuz it's the best one."

I set the bag of food on the floor and slide my boots on. "You're not wrong there," I say, smiling at his excitement. "I'm going to head out, but thanks for the cookies again, and thank you for letting me come to dinner. Your mom makes the best meatloaf—you're a lucky kid." I catch Morgan standing at the doorway wiping her eyes discreetly. I shoot her a small smile and a nod. I'm not sure what has her upset, but she doesn't look like she wants to tell me either.

"Same time next week," she says. "Liam, go brush your teeth while I walk Mr. Brant out, please."

"Bye, Mr. Brant," Liam shouts, racing down the small hallway toward what I am guessing is the bathroom.

"Bye, kid. Be good for your mom." I reach for the door, bag in hand. "Bye, Morgan. Thank you for the best meal I've had in a long time." My eyes are drawn to her very kissable lips. I lean forward a bit, and then catch myself. This isn't a date, and Morgan certainly does not want a goodnight kiss. No matter how badly I want to find out if her lips are as soft as they look.

"Good night, Brant," Morgan says quietly. I step out onto the porch, the cool of the evening fall air sends goosebumps skittering down my arms.

"Night." I wait until I hear the lock slide into place and make my way to my truck. What the heck is happening? I'm drawn to her in a way I've never been drawn to anyone else. Is it just because she is a single mom with a little boy? Is it just compassion—a connection from my own childhood? I don't know, but I intend to figure it out.

Chapter Five

Morgan

THE LOCK SLIDES INTO place, firmly securing a much-needed barrier between us. I didn't expect him to be so thoughtful. William was amazing, but he never helped with the dinner dishes. He always plopped on the sofa and turned on the T.V. after we ate.

Rubbing my hand down my arm, I remember the tingling sensation of Brant's strong arm brushing against mine. Dropping my hand, I shake my head. I have no time for dating. Guilt gnaws at me; how could I even be feeling anything toward another man? I loved my husband. He was *it* for me. That doesn't just go away. Does it?

Splashing noises interrupt my guilt trip. I head down the hallway, pausing just outside the bathroom door. Liam has his toothbrush dangling from his mouth while he is splashing his favorite small red car through the water in the bottom of the sink.

"Liam, that is gross. You're getting toothpaste and spit all over the car." Shaking my head, I unplug the drain and watch the water drain from the sink. "Finish up, and rinse that car off, it needs to dry so it doesn't rust. Then it's bedtime, mister." I kiss the top of his head.

Hearing him talk about his dad's old toys reminds me again just how much William is missing out on. Liam may have his cars, but he won't have the memories of playing them with his dad. I worry that Liam won't remember William. He was so little when he died. Even though we talk about him, and his pictures still hang on our walls, I can see Liam's actual memories fading.

Wiping at my eyes, I grab Liam's favorite pajama set out of his dresser and lay it across his bed. I pick up the few toys littering the space and place them back into the bins. Liam's room is small, but tidy. He has a bookshelf with bins of toys, a small desk to color on, and a bit of space on the floor to play. What more could a little boy need?

Liam comes charging in, car and face wet with water. "I rinsed it, Mom. It's all clean. Can I sleep with it?" Seeing his pjs, he quickly scrambles out of his clothes and into his pajama pants.

"It's wet and needs to dry, remember? How about we put it on a towel next to your bed, and it can sleep there?" I ask. Reaching for the pajama top, I hold it up for him to stick his head and arms through.

"Okay, I guess so." He pouts, pulling down the shirt and climbing into his bed. "But can it sleep right here so I can see it?" he asks, pointing to the little space on the nightstand next to his spiderman night light.

"Sure, let me grab a towel."

Closing Liam's door gently, I let out a deep breath. What a day. Liam had a hard time falling asleep; three books, and twenty minutes of cuddling later, he is finally down.

Exhaustion weighs heavily on me tonight. Standing in the hallway, I look at the door to my room. William has been gone for two years, yet I still feel like I have betrayed him somehow. I've never been attracted to another man before, but I can't deny Brant has my attention.

I was sure that part of me had died with William. How could anyone ever take his place? Liam deserves to know how much his parents loved each other. Now I am wondering if I am meant to stay single the rest of my life, or if there might just be a second chance at happiness for me. As I enter the room I shared with William, I wonder if the sadness will ever go away completely. How could I even think about Brant when I still hurt over the loss of my husband?

Grabbing my favorite flannel pajamas, I head into the bathroom. I am craving the warmth of a bubble bath tonight. Starting the water, slightly hotter than normal, I add in lavender bath oils and wait for it to fill. The scent of lavender mixes with the steam rising from the tub to cover the room in a calm soothing mist. Turning off the water, I slide into the bath up to my chin. The water, a bit too hot, turns my pale skin pink. Inhaling deeply, I focus on the scent of lavender and allow my muscles to relax.

My mind starts to wander. Brant's green eyes when I told him I was a widow, filled with so much compassion. His deep laughter, and genuine smile. For the first time, I allow myself to wonder what it would be like to have someone to come home to again. Someone to cook dinners with, clean up the messes with, tuck Liam into bed with.

Rationally, I know William is gone, and I am allowed to date again. I just haven't been ready. I don't think I am ready now. Not really, but it feels closer than it ever has before.

The screeching buzz of the alarm jolts me awake. My heart is racing out of my chest. I take a deep breath, and then another. Stupid alarm. I have the sense I was dreaming the most magnificent dream. It's been three weeks since that first dinner with Brant, which means three weeks' worth of Brant dreams. This one's still there—it's foggy, just out of reach, but it has left a warm happy impression behind.

Blasted alarm.

Throwing the covers back, I roll out of bed. Morning comes too soon when sleep comes so late. Rubbing the grit out of my eyes, I make my way to the bathroom to start my morning routine. After William died, I created a little list I followed so I didn't forget anything. Now it's a habit. Brush my teeth, wash my face, comb my hair, moisturize, and make up. It's almost a jingle now. I throw on a pair of black slacks and a blouse with huge tulips on it. I may teach pre-k, but I don't have to dress like Ms. Frizzle to do it.

Wearing nice clothes always helps me feel more in-control of my day. Something about that saying "look nice, feel nice" has really stuck with me. Plus, it's a lot easier to fool myself into thinking I have it all together if I don't feel frumpy.

"Liam, time to get up," I shout, walking past his door. "Your breakfast will be ready in a minute, and we have to leave for school." Hearing a loud groan from his room, I smile. I wonder if his teen years will be tough, considering he already hates waking up in the morning.

Heading into the kitchen, I make my way to the counter and start the coffee pot. Strong, dark, and hot, the best way to start the day. Brant pops into my mind suddenly. I guess he fits that description too. I giggle to myself while I get down my travel mug.

The last few weeks have been nice. I've enjoyed having another adult to talk to in the evening. Brant has brought Liam a little something every week, and, despite my protests, he helps me clean the kitchen before we play a few rounds of cards. We talk about everything and nothing at the same time. We are both yawning before we are ready to say goodnight and Brant heads home.

I find myself wondering what it would feel like to kiss his soft-looking lips. To feel his hands wrap around me for more than a fleeting hug. Shaking my head, I get to work packing sandwiches and making Liam's breakfast of microwaved oatmeal. I don't have time to daydream this morning.

"Mommy," Liam growls. "I don't wanna go to school today. I wanna play with my cars some more." He is rubbing one eye and dragging his feet. One sock barely holding on. His little shirt is buttoned up wrong, making little pockets poke up off his chest.

"I know, but Mrs. Delaney will miss you if you aren't there today. Plus, isn't today your music day? You love music class." Pulling him gently toward me, I fix the buttons on his shirt and try to press down the hair that is sticking up every which way. "Here, sit down and eat your breakfast. You'll feel better with something warm in your belly."

Liam sits grumpily on the chair, one leg swinging back and forth off the side. Grabbing a spoon, he digs in, taking huge mouthfuls. "Slow down Liam, you'll choke." It's a refrain I have to say all too often.

He shoots me an apologetic grin and starts taking smaller bites. Satisfied he is eating and dressed, I shoot to my room to grab my shoes and my bag. If we don't leave soon, we'll be late. Again.

I hear Liam put his bowl in the sink and head into the bathroom. The sound of the water coming on makes me smile. Routine. We thrive on it.

I bump into him coming down the hallway. "Sorry, bud, you okay?" I ask, wiping a smudge of toothpaste off the corner of his mouth.

"Can I take my car to school today? Please? I'll keep it in my backpack," Liam pleads, his dark brown puppy dog eyes trained on me.

"You can take it in the car, but it will have to stay there until after school. You're not allowed to take toys to class, and I'm sure you don't want to lose your favorite car." Raising an eyebrow, I cock my head to the side the way I've always imagined moms do when they mean business. I am not a good negotiator. Too many times since his father died I've given in without much of a fight. He's still a good kid though.

This time, he doesn't argue. Just nods his little head and runs down the hall.

"Meet me at the door, it's time to go!" I say as he turns the corner into his room. "Yes, Mom," Liam shouts back.

We make it to school with minutes to spare. Every single morning is a rush against the clock. Sometimes I wish I'd picked a different profession, but then I wouldn't get to spend as much time with Liam.

Grabbing my coffee, I rush down the hallway, dropping Liam off in his class before booking it to my classroom. Turning a corner, I barely avoid getting knocked over by a ball barreling down the hallway. "Watch out, boys. No kicking balls in the hall." Shaking my head, I slide into my classroom right on time. My co-teacher, Reese, shakes her head and smiles.

"Morgan, I wasn't sure you'd make it in time." She laughs. The kids are already seated around the tiny tables with their morning coloring sheets in front of them. "So, late night?" She grins and waggles her eyebrows.

Shaking my head, I roll my eyes at her ridiculousness. "No, actually, I was in bed right on time." I shoot her a discouraging look. "Alone," I whisper so little ears don't hear. Reese has been my co-teacher since I started in the pre-k classroom. She's four years younger than I am, and still playing the dating game—all hopeless optimism and big dreams of a "happily ever after."

"Darn, I was hoping Mr. Mechanic might just break your lug nuts loose." She cackles, moving away from me when a student raises their hand.

The rest of the day passes fairly quickly. Even the afterschool shift I picked up is pretty tame compared to usual. Normally kids are wild after being cooped up at their desks most of the day, but the weather has been unusually nice, so the teachers are letting their classes stay outside a bit longer in the afternoons.

Slinging my bag over my shoulder, I wave goodbye to Lucy, the fifth grade teacher who stayed this afternoon. "C'mon, Liam, let's go home." I grab his little backpack and take his hand as we walk to the car.

Unlocking the car, I open his door first, letting him scoot in to start buckling himself up. I reach over and toss my bag into the front passenger seat, and check to make sure his straps are tight. Kissing his head, I close his door and slide into the driver seat. Exhausted, I take a moment to let out a breath and just sit.

"How was your day?" I ask, clipping my seatbelt into place and looking over my shoulder. "Did you have fun in music class?"

Liam raises one little shoulder. "I guess." He yawns. Little dark circles under his eyes give away just how hard it was for him to fall asleep last night. "Can we go see Mr. Brant? I want to ask him something about my car." Liam is already racing the car back and forth across his leg and up the side of his booster seat.

"Mr. Brant is busy today. Besides, we need to get home and have some dinner. It will be bedtime before you know it." Making my way slowly out of the parking lot. I glance in the rear-view mirror. Liam's face is one big pout. "We'll see Mr. Brant again next week when he comes over for dinner."

He shrugs his shoulders again and turns to look out the window. The light turns green, and I hit the gas, anxious to be home. Halfway under the light I hear a loud honking noise and screeching tires. I look to my left to see a large truck careening through the intersection right towards us. Jerking the wheel, I try to angle my car so that the impact is as far away from Liam as possible, then the sickening sound of metal on metal, followed by a sharp pain in my forehead... and darkness takes over.

CHAPTER SIX

Brant

My heart is in my throat. Panic hits me like a ton of bricks. I barely get the truck in park as I jump out and race toward Morgan's crumpled car. "Someone call 9-1-1!" I scream. Pushing past the driver of the truck that rammed her, I run right to her door and try to open it, but it's locked. Her body is slumped over the steering wheel, the deflated airbag hanging limply in front of her. I can't tell if she is hurt, but I can see she is still breathing.

Forcing myself to stay calm, I look to the back seat. Liam is buckled into his seat sobbing. Sound comes rushing into my ears like the world was on mute and someone turned the volume back on.

Sirens blare as they make their way to the scene. Liam's door is locked too. Running back to my truck, I grab my multi-tool flashlight from under the front seat and race back to Morgan's car. Using the pointed glass-breaker end of the flashlight, I smash in the window furthest from Liam, reach in and unlock the door. Climbing through the shattered glass, I reach out for Liam's hand.

"It's okay, bud, I'm here." I keep my voice calm and try to determine if he's injured. "Does anything hurt, Liam? Are you hurt?"

I look to where Morgan is now moaning softly. That's a good sign, right? I turn back to Liam; tears are running down both his little cheeks. Carefully, I wipe his eyes. "Mommy! Mommy! Wake Up!" Liam is screaming now, panic making his voice louder than I have ever heard a little kid be.

"Listen, Liam," I say calmly. My insides twist and fear grips my throat, making it hard to speak. "Look, the firemen are here. They made it. See? They're going to come help your mom and you now." I hold his little hand and hope to God I'm not wrong. Spotting his favorite red car on the floorboard, I lean down and snag it. He'll want this when he calms down, I'm sure.

"But..." His little body rocks from the force of his crying. "But the firemans couldn't save my daddy." He's crying even harder now. The firemen wrench open Morgan's door. I can see the paramedic reach in to take her vitals.

"We have a pulse, but she's unconscious. We need a stretcher over here." The paramedic reaches over and undoes her seatbelt as another man opens Liam's door and ducks his head in. "Are you the dad?" he asks.

"No, a family friend." Before he can even question it I add, "I'm staying. I'm staying with them."

The paramedic gives a quick nod and turns his attention to Liam. After checking him out, they decide to take him to the hospital too as a precaution. As they unstrap him and pull him out of the car seat, and away from me, the EMT says, "Follow behind the ambulances; we'll meet you at the hospital ER. I'm sorry there isn't room to have you ride along safely." I want to protest that I should ride with Liam, but I don't. My heart is lodged in my throat, and the only thing I can think is that they have to be okay.

"Liam, I'll be right behind you, okay? You're safe, I promise." Turning, I take off for my truck. Shaking, I yank the handle and jump in. Reaching into my pocket I drag out my phone. My hands are shaking so badly I drop the phone twice before I manage to dial the number.

"Hello, Brant's Automotive."

I take a breath trying to get myself together. "Daniel, it's Brant. Listen, I need you to call the parts store and have them deliver those gaskets, and I need you to close up the shop for me." My voice sounds strange to my own ears, like it's in one of those weird echo chambers at a fair.

"I hear sirens," Daniel says. "You okay, man? What happened? You sound shaken up." Daniel has worked for me since I opened the shop. He knows me better than anyone. At this point, he is the closest thing to family I have.

"Yeah, I'm fine. I happened to be passing by the school and saw Morgan's car get t-boned." My voice hitches. She has to be all right.

Daniel sucks in a breath. "How is she? Was Liam with her?" Daniel used to work in a body shop. He's seen the damage an accident can cause.

"She was unconscious at first, but she was restless and moaning when they were closing the doors to the ambulance." I take a shuddering breath. "Liam looks fine, just shaken up. They took him too, just to be safe." I put him on speaker and turn the truck around. "Listen, I'm not sure if I'll be in tomorrow, but you've got this. I'll call you later. I've got to get to the hospital." My heart is still racing, and I know the adrenaline drop will be rough.

Daniel says something about having it under control, but I don't hear him. My mind is already at the hospital.

I make it to the ER in record time and pull my truck into the first available space. I'm out and running through the sliding doors. I make my way to the check-in desk. A young girl with strawberry blond hair is manning the computers. "Morgan Prescott," I gasp. "She and her son were brought in by ambulance—where are they?"

Bethany, according to the name tag pinned to her pink and blue striped scrubs, looks up at me with a bored expression. "Are you family?" she asks, typing something on the keyboard I hope will tell me where Morgan and Liam are.

"Yes," I don't have time for red tape. "I'm her fiancée." The lie rolls off my tongue like I say it every day.

"Liam is in room three. Morgan is beside him in room four. I don't know anything else." She prints out a visitor sticker and buzzes me through.

"Thanks," I spit out, already rushing toward the opening doors.

Finding room three first, I brace myself. Liam is probably terrified. The last thing he needs to see is someone freaking out. I hate that I wasn't with him in the ambulance. Grabbing hold of the door, I twist the handle and step inside.

"Mr. Brant!" Liam yells, hopping down from the table and throwing himself into my legs. "Mommy waked up, but she didn't feel so good." Tears slide down his little face.

The nurse is watching us with a gentle smile and says, "Liam wouldn't calm down until he saw his mom, so we had them in the same room for a bit. We brought him in here when they took her back for tests. Mom gave us the go ahead to release him to either a Susan Mathews, or Brant Anderson."

"I'm Brant Anderson," I say pulling out my ID and showing it to her. Reaching down, I lift Liam up and hold him to my chest, my eyes damp. "See, the helpers were there." I choke out the words. The nurse moves from the corner of the room and pats Liam on the leg.

"Liam has been checked over. He will probably be sore tomorrow and will have a bruise from the car seat straps, but he is physically fine," she says. "Thank goodness he's still in a five point harness, or this could have been a lot worse."

She taps some papers on the counter and lays my ID on the top. "We were able to find him in the system, so his insurance is already processed. It's a good thing Mom was conscious—his emergency contact hasn't been updated since his father passed away. Here are his discharge papers." She gives me a small smile. "He has been talking about you since he got here."

I hold him a little tighter. When did this little guy bury himself so deeply into my heart? "Thank you. How is his mom?" I ask, the plea in my voice clear as day.

"They took her down for imaging, she should be back up soon. She's in a lot of discomfort, but she is awake." She smiles softly and ruffles Liam's hair. "It's slow this afternoon, you two can stay here while we wait for some more information." She nods to me, and heads into the hallway.

"Where is room four? Where is Morgan?" a frantic sounding woman is yelling at the nurses' station. Still holding Liam, I step to the door.

"Do you know her?" I ask Liam quietly at the same time the crazed woman looks our way.

"Liam!" She rushes to us. "Liam, thank goodness you're all right." She looks at me for the first time, her dark blue eyes brimming with tears. Now I recognize her. Susan, the friend who brought Morgan to pick up her car.

"You must be Brant. How did you get here so fast? I only just found out from Lucy. She saw the scene when she was leaving the school." She has barely taken a breath, and her face is stained with tears. "She would have come, but she had to get her teenager to work." Susan wrings her hands together. "How is she? Where is she?"

Susan may be small, but she is putting off some serious protector vibes. I take a breath and try to remember all of her questions. "I was driving by on my way to the parts store. I saw the whole thing happen and followed them to the hospital." I shift Liam to my side, not ready to put him down. "Morgan is down for imaging. Liam is fine—he was actually just discharged. The nurse said we can wait here until the doctor is ready to talk to us."

Rubbing Liam's back, she looks up at me. "Thank God you were there. I'm Susan, by the way."

I put out my hand to shake hers. She looks at my hand and leans in and hugs me. "I've heard a lot about you," she whispers. Stunned, I forget to speak for a moment. I finally nod and set Liam down on the exam table.

An hour later, we're crammed into Morgan's room waiting for the doctor to come tell us the results of the images. They've started an IV and given her some pain medicine. She is fading in and out of sleep, but for the first time since seeing her car get hit, I can breathe normally.

Her lip is split, and bruises are setting in on her face. Her hair, normally so put together, is all tangled. My heart aches for her, but I can't help but think that, even in this state, she is the most beautiful woman I've ever seen.

Liam is sitting with Susan, happily munching on chips and taking sips of apple juice we found in the vending machine at the end of the hall. Susan is reading a book she found in the waiting area when we went to get Liam a snack. Something about a blue truck and Christmas.

A knock on the door has us all holding our breath. An older man steps into the room and takes a look around. "Hello," he says. "I'm

Dr. Everett. I have Morgan's results here." Moving to the bed, he puts on his stethoscope and presses it to her chest. "She suffered a concussion from the airbag. She also has a broken ankle, and a few broken ribs. We'll keep her overnight for observation, but if all goes well, she should be able to go home tomorrow. She'll need some help for a few days until she can move around well on her own. Someone will be in shortly to move her to a room."

He shakes my hand, and nods to Susan before leaving the room.

"I can take Liam home with me. I have a car seat in my car still from when we dropped Morgan's car off," Susan says. "I hate leaving her here alone like this." She sighs, hugging Liam close to her.

"I want to stay with Mommy," Liam says, his face wrinkling and tears brimming his eyes. "I want to stay here." He pushes off of Susan's lap and runs to me, throwing his arms around my neck. "I want to stay here," he repeats through his sobs.

"Liam," I say softly, rubbing his back. "How about I make you a deal?" I wait for him to nod. "I'll stay here with your mom, and you go home with Ms. Susan. Tomorrow, I'll bring your mommy home, and we can stay together there until your mom is feeling better." Keeping my arms wrapped around his little body, which is shaking with every breath, I try to soothe him the best I can.

"You'll stay here?" he says, his bottom lip quivering with the effort it's taking him to calm down. "You won't leave mommy by herself?"

I pull back from him and stick out my hand to shake on it. "I promise," I say. Liam shakes my hand and drops his head. Shuffling his feet, he makes his way back across the room to where Susan is now standing. "All right, we can go," he says, taking a last look at his mom. "Bye, Mommy, I'll see you tomorrow."

My heart breaks for this little guy. I can't imagine how he must be feeling, having already lost his dad. "She hears you, little man," I say. "I'll take care of her."

The steady sound of Morgan's breathing is the only thing keeping me sane. In and out, a reminder that she is still here and will be okay. I break down after Liam leaves, letting the emotions come full force. After several minutes, I'm able to get it together. Taking out my phone, I decide to give Daniel a call. Things just got a whole lot more complicated.

"Hey, Brant, how's it going? Any word?" Daniel asks as soon as he picks up the phone.

I rub my hand down the side of my face, the dried tears making my skin feel gritty. "Hey, they said she has a broken ankle, some broken ribs, and a concussion. They are keeping her overnight, but they let Liam go home with Morgan's friend." Looking over at Morgan in the hospital bed, my heart squeezes in my chest. "I'll need a few days off. Think you can handle it?" I know he can, but I've never left for more than a day or two at a time.

"Evan and I have the shop covered. Don't even worry about that," he says. "How are you holding up?" Over the last few weeks, Daniel has been encouraging me to make a move. I usually shake my head and tell him he is crazy, but his instinct is right. I have developed feelings for her, and I don't want to waste any more time. Today is a reminder that life is short, and I'm done pretending like she and Liam aren't everything that is missing in my life.

"Not gonna lie, this was terrifying. I've never been so scared in all my life. When I saw her slumped over, all I could think about were the last few weeks, playing cards with her after dinner, talking about everything and nothing. I want that, Daniel, and I saw it being taken from me before I ever had a chance to tell her how I feel."

Letting out a deep breath, I choke up as I take in the bruises that are covering Morgan's face. "The car took a huge hit, and by the time I got there, Morgan was out, face in the airbag." Tears threaten the backs of my eyes.

"That sounds awful. It's a good thing you were there. I can't imagine how Liam felt." Daniel has a daughter of his own, so I know he understands how intense this situation has been.

"He was scared. His dad died from a heart attack a few years ago. From what I understand, he doesn't really remember it well, but he knows the basics." I shudder, remembering the sound of his little screams. "He was pretty shaken up at first but was in a little better spirits when he left tonight, especially since I salvaged his favorite toy car." I sigh, looking over at the still-sleeping Morgan. She looks so small in the hospital bed with the monitors attached. I pull the covers up over her arms so she doesn't catch a chill. Hospitals are always so cold.

"I'm sure that helped. I'm glad he's okay," Daniel says. "I couldn't imagine anything like that happening to my Elli."

"He is a good kid. He made me promise to stay here with Morgan so she isn't alone." Standing, I pace the room, needing something to do besides sit and relive the accident over and over again.

"What happens when she is discharged?" Daniel asks. "Is she going to stay with her friend?"

"Nah, I told Liam I would come stay with them—if it's all right with his mom, that is. She really doesn't like asking for help." I chuckle and run my hand over the back of my neck, gently rubbing some of the tension away.

Daniel chuckles. "You sure about that, man? Seems like you're already in pretty deep."

"I figured Liam would be more comfortable at home, and I already know Morgan doesn't like accepting help. Probably easier for her if she's in her own home. Susan is a teacher too—I don't know her family situation, but I imagine she can't take a ton of time off of work. That's two teachers they'd have to find substitutes for." *That's my story and I'm sticking to it.* It has nothing to do with the fact that even the thought of not being there for her right now makes me sick to my stomach.

"I know I've been giving you a hard time about asking her out, or telling her you like her, but I gotta tell you, if this isn't a wakeup call…" He trails off.

"Yeah, I know," I say. "I'm just not sure she's ready to hear it." I stretch my arms over my head balancing the phone on my shoulder. "If I don't know how she feels yet, how can I tell her I'm falling in love with her?"

A gasp has me spinning around. "Uh, shoot. Gotta go. I'll call you tomorrow," I say, hanging up without giving Daniel a chance to say goodbye. My face falls in my hands and I take a few deep breaths before I turn around. How much had she heard?

"Morgan," I say nervously. "How are you feeling? Do you want me to get the nurse?" I start towards the door to flag down the night nurse. "Are you hungry?"

"Brant." Her voice scratches as she tries to speak. "Brant, did you mean it?" Stopping mid stride, I lower my head. My heart is beating out of my chest. I didn't mean for her to hear me. Slowly I turn around and make my way to her bedside. Carefully, I lift her hand in mine.

"Morgan, I know you aren't ready, and I don't want to rush you," I say, pausing to gather my courage. "But I meant it. Somehow these last few weeks, I've developed feelings for you, and for Liam. Seeing you guys in that accident today almost killed me." I wipe the hair back from her face, resisting the urge to lean down and kiss the bruise just below her eye.

"I—" She stops. "Brant, I don't know what to say." She tries to adjust her position in the bed and grimaces. "I'm not sure..."

"Don't say anything," I whisper, cutting her off before she can finish that thought. I press my lips to her forehead. "Now isn't the time." Standing back, I lay her hand back at her side. "I'm going to get the nurse now. It's probably time for your medicine."

Stretching my neck from side to side, I stand, trying to work the kinks out of my back. Sleeping in a hospital chair is not good for the body. I eye the hard reclining chair the nurse pulled in for me last night when I made it clear I was not leaving. The thin blanket and barely filled pillow did nothing to make me more comfortable, but I was here, and that's what matters.

Thankfully, Morgan seems to be resting peacefully. A soft knock sounds at the door. "Hey, is anyone awake?" Daniel peeks his blond head through the door. The aroma of coffee has my tired brain perking up. "I brought some breakfast." He lifts a paper bag.

"Hey," I whisper. "She's out, but come on in. Coffee sounds amazing right now." Yawning, I clear a space on the small rolling table for him to place the cup holder and bag he's carrying. The sugary sweet smell of donuts mixes with the strong smell of donut-shop coffee promising a hit of caffeine and warmth. Why do they always keep it so cold in hospitals?

"How's she doing?" Daniel asks, grimacing as he takes in her bruised face and the cast running halfway up her calf. "She looks rough." Shaking his head, he gives me a sympathetic look.

"She's hurting, but she's strong," I say taking a sip of the too-hot coffee. "It'll be a rough few days, but she'll be all right." Prying off the lid of the coffee cup, I inhale deeply. There is nothing like the smell of coffee in the morning.

"Well, I just wanted to swing by and check on things, bring you some decent food. I wasn't sure you'd leave her to go get anything to eat." He stares at me pointedly and I shrug in response. "I'm headed to the shop to open up. Let me know if you need anything." Daniel grabs his own cup out of the tray and takes a sip.

"Thanks, D, I appreciate it. You're a lifesaver." I mean it. Daniel and I have been through a lot together these last five years. If there is anyone I trust to run the shop while I'm out, it's him.

He nods and quietly makes his way toward the door. "No problem. Take your time coming back. We've got it covered," he says, slipping out the door and quietly closing it behind him.

Glancing at the still-sleeping Morgan, I start to wonder what it would be like to cut back my hours some and spend more time with her and Liam. I can see us spending time in my backyard throwing a ball or chasing around a dog. Morgan with a baby on her hip. I wonder if she would want another child. I can't rush her, but I want it all.

With her.

Whatever she'll give me. But I'd also be happy if Liam is the only child we ever have in our lives. Now, if I can convince her to take a chance on letting me in, on loving again...

Chapter Seven

Morgan

Murmuring voices seep into my sleepy haze before the soft click of a door brings silence again. My eyes don't want to open, but the faint aroma of strong coffee pricks my nose. Yawning, I move to sit up. "Ung," I moan. Everything hurts. Taking a shallow breath, I try again.

"Wait," a deep voice says. "I'll help." Suddenly, warm hands are under my arms gently lifting me in the bed. I pry open my eyes and realize Brant is standing over me, his forehead wrinkled with concern. His emerald eyes hold mine. "You okay?" he asks.

Nodding my head, I move to press the button that lifts the head of the bed. "Do I smell coffee?" I inhale as deeply as my ribs will allow. "It smells so good."

My mouth feels like it's filled with cotton balls, my tongue is sticking to the roof of my mouth, and my head is pounding. The pain medicine must be wearing off.

Brant nods and points to the nearby table. "My friend Daniel stopped by with coffee and donuts." He smiles at me, brushing the hair from my face. "Would you like me to ask the nurse if you can have some?"

I shake my head gently. "No. I just want you to give it to me. I'll ask forgiveness later." Laughing, Brant pushes the cart further away.

"No can do, sweetheart, but I'll page the nurse and we can ask together."

A few minutes later, the nurse, Mona, comes in rolling her computer cart in front of her. "How are you feeling this morning, Morgan?" she asks, clipping the oxygen sensor onto my finger and taking my temperature with one of those forehead scanner things.

"I would be better if Brant would let me have some of that coffee he's hiding," I say accusingly.

Mona chuckles, typing my vitals into the computer.

"I'm okay, just really sore. It hurts to take a deep breath, and this cast is heavy," I say pointing to the foot of the bed. "My head is killing me, and everything hurts." I close my eyes and lay my head back.

"That's to be expected. You took quite a hit yesterday." Thankfully she hands me a little paper cup with some pills in it and a small cup of water. "These should help with the pain. The doctor will be by to check on you in a little bit. My guess is he'll send you home since you did so well overnight."

I dump the medicine into my mouth and swallow it down with the water. "Let me know if you need anything." She types some things into the computer and smiles at me. "I'll be back to check on you in a while," she says, turning and rolling her cart to the door.

"Wait!" I say louder than I intended too, making me cringe. "Coffee—can't I have some?" I beg.

Laughing, Mona opens the door. "You can eat and drink—just take it easy," she says and pushes her way into the hallway.

I turn and stick my tongue out at Brant. "See, I told you I could have the coffee," I say. Brant rolls the table closer to the bed and pops the lid off the to-go cup. Steam rises from the opening and my mouth starts to water. "I'll take a donut too, please," I say, looking up at him.

"Do you want glazed, or cake?" he asks. "Apparently, Daniel brought a few to choose from." He holds out the bag, letting me peek inside. Laying out a napkin, he reaches in and grabs one of each. "How about you eat what you want, and whatever you don't eat, I'll finish off?"

"Thanks, Brant," I say softly. I look around the small room, really taking it in for the first time since they transferred me here last night. Thankfully, I'm in a private room. The walls are painted a soft peach with pictures of flowers hung randomly on two of the walls. A whiteboard boasts the name of my nurse, the doctor, and a few other people, along with their phone extensions. A reclining chair sits next to my bed, and, from the pillow and blankets thrown haphazardly across it, I surmise he stayed the night.

"You didn't have to sleep in the chair. You could have gone home." Tears prick my eyes, and my throat clogs with emotion. "Thank you," I whisper. Suddenly, I feel very alone, even with Brant's presence. How am I going to teach, or take care of Liam, when I can't even sit myself up? Swiping at my wet cheeks, I tear a little piece off of the cake donut and pop it into my mouth.

"I promised Liam I wouldn't leave you alone. A man doesn't break promises like that if he can help it," he says, taking another sip of his coffee. "Besides, there's no place I would rather be."

Finished with the donuts, I slide what is left towards Brant and finally give voice to my fears. "How am I going to get to work? I'm assuming the car is totaled?" My eyes close. It may not have been the newest fanciest car, but it ran. "After all that work you put in to fix it, it's been running like a dream. And I still owe you all that money from the tires and belts." Reality has started to sink in, and the donuts I just ate threaten to revolt.

"Don't worry about any of that now," Brant says, taking my hand. "Susan called. She told the principal what happened. Mrs. Montgomery said to take all the time you need. As for the car..." He pauses. "Yeah, I'm sure it's totaled." He rubs his thumb across the back of my hand, causing goosebumps to skitter up my arm. "When we get you home today, I'll call the insurance company and see if we can get the ball rolling on the claim. I'll stay on the couch and help with Liam until you're feeling better. The doctor said it should only be a few days before you're able to get around a bit better on your own."

"What?" I shout, balling my fists at my sides. "How can you say don't worry? You have no idea what it is like to be a single mother. I can't just miss work. I'll run out of PTO. I need that time in case something happens with Liam. If he gets sick it's me that has to call out of work to stay home with him." I know he's trying to help, but I'm frustrated. "Brant, I appreciate you trying to help, but I'm on my own. I've got no one—I can't just not work. I don't have that option."

Taking a breath, I try to calm my racing heart. "I have no savings. Nothing. Liam wants to go trick-or-treating Sunday, and I can't even walk." My voice is rising and I can't stop it. "What am I going to do?" Putting my head in my hands, I let the tears fall. All the while, Brant rubs slow circles on my back.

"That's where you're wrong. I do know what it's like. My mom raised me all by herself after my dad died. I know it's hard. I'll help, Morgan. We'll figure it out. You're not alone. You have Susan, and you have me." He sounds so sincere, but he has no idea what it takes to keep things going in my life. Why does he have to be so darn nice?

A sharp knock on the door sounds before the doctor walks in. "Morgan, how are you feeling today?" he says, cleaning his hands.

I think for a minute, trying to steady my breath from my outburst. "I'm sore, but the medicine is helping with the pain for the most part. It hurts to move around much, or to take deep breaths, and my life is falling apart, but otherwise I'm great," I say morosely.

Leaning in, he places the stethoscope against my chest. "Take a few deep breaths for me." After a few minutes he stands back up. "Your lungs sound clear, so that is good. The imaging showed a slight concussion, so I'd like you to take it easy for the next few days. You can go back to work in a week if you're feeling up to it." He looks at Brant. "Will you be staying with her?"

"No," I say at the same time Brant says, "Yes."

Looking between the two of us the doctor says, "Morgan, you will need someone to help you for a few days. You're going to be really sore, even with pain medicine." He looks at Brant again. "Is there someone else you want me to call? Your parents maybe?"

Sighing, I shake my head. "No," I say. "There isn't anyone else." Looking at Brant, I realize I have no choice but to swallow my pride. "Thank you for offering to stay with me. Looks like I'll need your help after all."

Brant smiles kindly, like I didn't just rudely refuse his help and yell at him while he was being so nice to me. I feel like a total heel.

A few hours later, Mona rolls me down the hallway in a wheel-chair. "You'll need to pick up the crutches and your medicine from the pharmacy next to the hospital," she says, whisking me around corners and down the hallway. Brant has gone to move his truck to the patient pick-up area.

"Got it," I say through gritted teeth. Who knew broken ribs could hurt so much? For the first time, I'm thankful that William died quickly and didn't suffer. That thought hits me, and I start to sob uncontrollably. I'm so lucky that things weren't worse, but right now all I can feel is raw hurt. How could he die and leave me here on my own?

"Are you okay?" Mona asks, pushing me out the sliding doors where Brant is waiting by his truck.

"He died," I sob. "He died, and I didn't." The tears won't stop, and I can't get any more words out. The crying is making my ribs ache even more, trying to take a breath between sobs is causing fresh waves of pain to take hold.

Rushing to my side, Brant kneels down and takes my hands. "Her husband died a few years ago. I think it's all catching up to her," he says softly to the nurse. "I've got her."

I don't hear her response over the sound of my own crying. Gently, Brant places one arm below my knees, and one under my arms and lifts me from the wheelchair and into the waiting truck.

"You're okay, Morgan. You're here," he whispers, placing a soft kiss on my temple. "Liam needs you. I need you." He steps back and runs the seatbelt across my lap. Closing the door, he makes his way to the driver's side and climbs in. Once he's buckled, he reaches out and holds my hand. "Let it out, Morgan," he says softly.

And I do. I cry all the way home. Sadness, guilt, frustration, anger... Years of pent up emotions pour down my face. He's gone. He's gone, but I'm not. Finally, the tears start to slow as we pull into the driveway of the two-bedroom house William and I bought when we first moved here.

All the hopes and dreams we shared.

Gone.

Putting the truck in park, Brant looks over at me. "I can't imagine how you must be feeling. Cry if you need to. Yell, be angry. Whatever it takes for you to process this." Lifting my hand, he places a gentle kiss on my palm. "I'm here."

Getting out of the truck he walks around to my side. "I hope you don't mind," he says, opening my door and unbuckling my seat belt, "but I asked Susan to grab your medicine and the crutches when she brings Liam home after school."

Too tired to speak, I nod. What else can I do? It's not like I can go get them myself. Brant lifts me out of the truck like I'm a bag of groceries, not the curvy woman I am. "I can try to walk," I croak out, my voice raw from crying. "I know I'm heavy."

Brant just scoffs. "You are not heavy," he says angrily. "You're perfect, and you're not putting any weight on that ankle until the doctor says it's okay." He gently sits me on one of the front-porch rockers. "Do you have a spare key hidden somewhere? Unfortunately I didn't think to grab your keys from the accident." He looks down at his feet, like a schoolboy who has just been chastised.

"It's okay, Brant, I wouldn't have thought about keys either," I admit. "I have a spare on the back porch under the planter."

"I'll be right back." He turns, giving me the perfect view of his backside in his work pants. I realize then, he's still in the clothes he wore to work yesterday.

Guilt hits like a ton of bricks. He's been nothing but nice and helpful, staying with me at the hospital, offering to help me, and here I am being so mean and emotional. Why can't I just accept his help?

He comes around the corner holding the key out in front of him. "Found it," he says, smiling. Turning the key in the lock, Brant opens the front door and props it open. Standing, I take one hop in that direction before I'm met with a scowling Brant. "What do you think you're doing?" he growls. "No weight on that foot—you heard the doctor." Scooping me up in his arms, he walks me through the house and places me on the couch.

Grabbing the throw pillows, he places them under my cast and knee, propping my leg up. "If you'd rather, I can move you to the bedroom. I thought you might want to be out here when Liam comes home." He looks uncertain.

"This is good for now. Thank you," I say. "Brant..." I pause, gathering my courage. "I'm sorry. You've been nothing but nice, and I've been a complete bear to be around." Shame and guilt eat at me. "Really. Thank you. I have no idea what would have happened if you hadn't been there." Liam would have been alone and scared without Brant's solid, reassuring presence.

"I'm glad I was there, too," he says. "I'm going to step outside and call Daniel, see if he'll bring me some clothes and things after work." He spins on his heel and steps outside before I can say anything else. My eyes close, and I rest my head on the arm of the couch. I'm worn out. The emotional roller coaster of this day, coupled with the pain and pain meds, is too much for me to deal with. I'm thankful I have a bit of time to get it together before Liam gets home from school.

Chapter Eight

Brant

Seeing Morgan completely break down shattered my heart. She must have been holding on to all that emotion for a long time. I rub my hands through my hair. I feel so help-less. Her world is falling apart, and there isn't anything I can do to save her from the pain. Neither the physi-cal pain from the accident, nor the emotional pain of her past.

I've never felt this way about anyone before. Watching that accident was like watching my future being crushed. Maybe I should walk away and give her space... but she needs *someone*. Who am I kidding? I *need* to be that someone. I couldn't walk away if I tried. Not from her, nor from Liam. Pulling my phone out of my pocket, I dial the shop.

"Brant's Automotive," Daniel answers. "How can I help you?"

"Hey, D, it's me. Thanks again for breakfast."

"No problem, you guys out of there yet?" he asks. "Need anything?"

Taking a step away from the house, I make my way to the edge of the driveway. "Do you think you could stop by my house and grab a few things? I don't want to leave her alone quite yet."

"Of course, man. What do you need?"

I list off the things I need, and Daniel says he can get it together, no problem.

"Hey, one more thing," I say, hoping I can make this happen. "Do you know anyone who might have a wheelchair Morgan can borrow for a few days?" His sister is in the medical field, so if anyone has a connection, it's him.

"I'll ask around and see what I can find."

"Thanks man. I'll talk to you later." Hanging up the phone, I make my way back inside. Susan will be here with Liam in a little bit, and I want to get Morgan to eat something before he gets home. Stepping back through the front door, I see Morgan asleep on the couch, worry lines creasing her gorgeous face. I'm glad to see she's resting. Her body has been through so much.

Quietly I step through to the kitchen and open the pantry door. Thankfully, she has some easy-to-make things on hand, because I am not a chef. Steak and potatoes is my specialty. Everything else is grilled cheese and takeout. I snag a can of soup off the shelf and open it. Pouring it into a bowl, I pop it in the microwave, and look for some crackers to serve with it. The beep of the timer pulls me out of the pantry empty-handed. Finding a kitchen towel, I place the bowl on the counter and look for a spoon. I fill a glass with water, and carefully balance the bowl between my chest and my arm. I tiptoe into the living room and set the water and soup on the table. Brushing the hair off of her face, I lean down and gently speak her name.

Morgan's eyes snap open, and for a moment she looks confused.

"It's okay, you fell asleep for a bit. I made you some soup. I couldn't find any crackers, though," I say, helping her up to a sitting position.

"Thank you," she says, rubbing her eyes. "Uhm, Brant..." Pink spreads across her cheeks. "I need the bathroom." She points to her foot, and down the hall. "Can you help me to the door? I can do the rest," she squeaks.

"Oh," I say. "Yeah, sure. Hang on." Taking the blanket off of her legs, I drape it across the back of the couch. Helping her up, I put her arm over my shoulders and grab her waist. "Lean on me," I say. "Don't put weight on that other foot."

We take small steps, her leaning her weight on me, and hopping on her one good foot. "Susan will have the crutches here soon. That should help." We make it to the bathroom, and I help her inside. She grips the countertop.

"I'll be right outside. Just tell me when you're ready, and I'll come help you back to the couch." She nods, and I step into the hallway, closing the door to give her some privacy. I lean against the far wall and wait. When she opens the bathroom door, I gently grab her around the waist and help her hobble back to the couch and settle in. "Susan should be here soon," I say. "She can help you change into something more comfortable. I'm sure you want out of those clothes."

I wait for Morgan to get comfortable before handing her the bowl of soup. "What do you think you might want for dinner?" I ask. "I can't really cook, but I order a mean takeout."

Blowing on the soup, Morgan lets out a quiet laugh. "I'm up for anything," she says. "But maybe we should let Liam choose, if you don't mind."

"Of course." I smile. "Is there anything you want me to do?" Being idle is not something I'm great at. It's why I've always loved working on cars. There's always a problem to solve, and something to do. I never even considered a desk job.

"How about you just sit with me and talk?" Morgan places her bowl back on the table in front of her. "We haven't really spent much time alone just talking," she says, reaching for the blanket on the back of the couch and wrapping it around her legs. "And I don't think I'm up for a game of cards."

"Sure," I say, sinking down into the overstuffed armchair. "What do you want to talk about?"

"Well..." Morgan shifts, making herself more comfortable. "Why did you open the auto shop? We haven't talked about that yet."

"I was never good at sitting still as a kid. My mom would get calls to come to the school for parent-teacher meetings all the time." I chuckle. "I got my first car at sixteen after saving money from cutting lawns for three summers, and it was a huge piece of junk. I started to work on it, slowly putting it back to rights as I had the money, and I fell in love with the process of taking something broken and making it run again." I shrug my shoulders. "I opened my own shop because I watched my mom struggle my whole life, and I didn't want to start a family and then struggle to take care of them. I wanted to have something I knew I could be good at, and that would allow me to provide for a family someday."

Morgan nods. "I never imagined struggling like this either. Being a single mom isn't easy. I do the best I can, but there is never enough money or time to do it all. I miss having William around to help with things." She looks down at her hands.

"I can understand that. My dad died when I was little. It was just my mom. She never remarried either. I think she was afraid to let someone else in," I say hesitantly. This is a touchy subject, and the last thing I want to do is upset Morgan again. "I only ever wanted her to be happy."

She leans back and closes her eyes for a minute. "It's hard to let go," she whispers, raising her eyes to mine. "I know he's gone, but I don't know how I can love someone else when I still love and miss him so much."

My heart shatters at her words. I knew she still loved him, but hearing her say she wonders how she could ever love again hurts. I nod, unable to speak for a moment. Clearing my throat, I lean forward. "I don't think you ever stop loving him, Morgan. I think you just make room to love someone new too, and if he's worth it, he will understand." Pushing myself to stand, I head for the front door. Suddenly I need some fresh air. "I'm going to be right outside."

A few minutes later, car tires crunch on the gravel drive. Hopping up from the rocking chair, I step down off the porch to meet Susan and Liam at her car.

"Mr. Brant!" Liam shouts, climbing out of his booster seat. "You stayed!" He runs forward, slamming his little body into my legs and wrapping his arms around me.

"Of course I did," I say. "A man has to keep his promises." I lean down and scoop him up, holding him close to me. "How was school today?"

"It was okay," he says, laying his head on my shoulder. "I was worried about Mommy all day. Can we go see her now?" he asks, already squirming to be let down.

I set him on the ground and kneel down. "Mommy is inside. You can go see her but be gentle—she is still a little bit hurt." Liam nods his head and then takes off down the walkway and into the house.

"Thanks a bunch," I say to Susan, reaching into the trunk to grab the crutches. "I appreciate you picking this stuff up. I just wanted to get her home and settled before Liam got home this afternoon."

"No problem. I'm glad I was able to help. How is she doing?" Susan closes the trunk and grabs the medicine bag out of the front seat before closing the door and following me up the walk.

"She's in pain, but she's a trooper. Frustrated and upset more than anything, I think." Susan is her best friend, and I know Morgan will need someone to talk to. "Do you want to stick around for dinner? Takeout," I say quickly. "I'm going to let Liam pick."

"Why don't I handle dinner, and you can run home and get whatever you need. Take a shower, check on your shop," she says. "Get some fresh air, I can stay until you're back. It will give me some time to help Morgan shower and get more comfortable."

"Are you sure? I was going to have my friend drop some stuff off, but I would rather choose my own clothes, to be honest. He's horrible at matching." I laugh. Once inside, I stow the crutches against the wall by the couch, and take the medicine bag from Susan and place it in the kitchen. "Do you want me to order dinner before I go?" I ask.

"Don't worry about it," Susan says. "I'll order in a bit. You like pizza?" She looks to Liam. "It's for sure what Liam will choose."

"Pizza is fine." I look at Morgan. "Do you need anything before I head out for a bit?"

She shakes her head. "I think I'm okay. When am I due for more medicine?" she asks, grimacing slightly as she shifts on the couch.

"In an hour. I put the medicine on the counter by the microwave," I say more to Susan than to Morgan.

"Okay," she tries to smile. "Take your time. I'll be here." Her attempt to make a joke falls flat when she lets out a whimper.

"Go," Susan says. "I've got her."

Nodding, I wave to Liam, who is playing with his cars on the floor, and head out the front door. I make my way to the shop to let Daniel know I don't need him to run by the house. I don't feel the need to check in, really. I'm sure he and Evan have it covered.

Pulling into my spot on the side of the building, I can see them standing over the engine bay of an older sedan. "What do we have here boys?" I ask loudly. Daniel jumps, not expecting my voice, I'm sure.

"Hey, man. How's your girl?" Evan asks, wiping his hands on a cloth he pulled from his pocket.

"She is just a friend," I remind them. "But she's doing okay. A fighter," I say softly. I wish I could call her my girl, but we definitely aren't there yet.

"I didn't think I'd see you until I dropped your stuff off later," Daniel says, eyeing me. He's been a single dad for so long, he has that suspicious eye thing down pat.

"Susan is with Morgan while I run out for a bit. I figured you probably had better things to do tonight than to grab my stuff." I shrug.

He stares at me a minute like he is trying to read my mind. "Elli is with her mom this week, so I'm free as a bird, but I'm glad I don't have to dig through your underwear drawer." He laughs.

"Aw, c'mon," Evan says, smiling. "You don't want to get up close and personal with his boxers?"

I shake my head. "You two are asking for it." They are, but I don't know what I'd do without them. They are the hardest workers I've ever known, and they're my best friends.

"Were you able to find anyone with a wheelchair I could borrow? Liam will want to go trick-or-treating, and there is no way Morgan is up for hobbling around the neighborhood in her condition."

Daniel shakes his head. "Nah, I tried, but I don't know who else to call."

Evan holds up his hand. "I might," he says. "Let me make a phone call." He steps away and takes his phone out of his pocket. He is on the phone a few minutes before coming back smiling. "My mom has one in her garage from when my Granddad was staying with us a while back. She said you can swing by and get it. She's putting it on her front porch for you right now."

Grinning, I clap him on the shoulder. "Remind me to give you a raise," I say, chuckling.

"Hey!" Daniel yells. "Don't forget about me, bossman!"

Evan gives me the address to his mom's, and I head back to the truck ready to grab my things and surprise Morgan and Liam with a solution to the trick-or-treating problem. I may not be able to solve all of her problems, but I can solve this one.

Chapter Nine

Morgan

I LAY MY HEAD back on the couch and groan. This whole situation is too much. "Thanks for bringing my medicine," I say to Susan. Lifting my head, I look to where Liam is playing on the floor. "I don't know how I'm going to do it all."

Susan follows my gaze. "He's a great kid," she says with a sigh. "He'll be all right. The important thing is that you recover." Standing, she grabs my empty water glass. "I'll go fill this up and be right back." Liam jumps up when she leaves the room and carefully sits by me on the couch.

"I missed you," I say, gently ruffling the top of his head. "How was your sleepover with Ms. Susan?" Liam rarely stays other places, but he has stayed with Susan a few times before when I've needed a break.

"It was fun. She made chicken for dinner, and little trees." He wiggles and I try not to let out any noise. The shifting on the couch sends shooting pain through my ribs and down through my ankle.

"I took a grown-up shower, and then—" He catches his breath. "And then, I slept on the floor! This morning I got to have waffles."

He pauses, his face lighting up. "Can I sleep on the floor tonight, Mommy?" In his excitement, he doesn't wait for me to respond. He jumps up from the couch, making me shift uncomfortably. "I can get my stuff!" He races down the hallway to his room and is out of sight. I'm glad he misses the grimace on my face.

I guess he can sleep on the floor tonight. There are worse ways he could be handling this.

Susan comes back into the room carrying the now full water glass and my medicine. "We thought he could use a distraction, so we made him a pallet on the floor of the living room." She smiles. "I slept on the couch so he wouldn't be alone." She sits the water glass in front of me, and pops open the medicine bottle. Pouring a pill into my palm, she closes the bottle, and hands me the water. "Go ahead and take that. It's time."

"Thanks," I mutter, grateful for the impending relief.

She heads to the kitchen. "I'm going to call for pizza," she says. "Which of these places delivers?" She turns the corner with several pizza brochures fanned out in her hand. "These all look the same to me." Sitting down on the couch beside me, she adjusts the pillow behind my back. "Pepperoni?"

I grab the flier for the pizza place Liam loves and hand it to her. "Sounds good."

Thirty minutes later, Liam is sprawled out in the pile of blankets he has thrown onto the floor. He's got pizza in his lap, and a juice box beside his makeshift bed. Susan has turned on his favorite superhero show, and he is happily in his own world.

"Thank you," I say. "For everything." I've barely eaten one piece, but it's all I can choke down. Pushing the plate away, I lean back and adjust the pillows. I'm exhausted, but I don't want to go to sleep until Liam does.

"That's what friends are for." Susan puts her empty plate under mine and wipes her hands on the napkin in her lap. "Listen," she starts. "I know it's been a lot, and I'm sure it's brought some painful memories to the surface…" She pauses, waiting for me to react.

I nod for her to continue. "You've been spending a lot of time with Brant these last few weeks. The way you talk about him makes me think you're starting to develop some real feelings, but if you don't want him to stay here and help, you just say the word."

A tear slides down my face, and I shake my head. "It's okay," I say softly. Just knowing she cares enough to offer is enough. She really is my best friend. "I could use your help with a shower, though, and some fresh clothes."

"You got it." Susan stands and helps me to my feet. "Liam, I'm going to help Mommy take a quick shower. You play here, okay? No going outside or opening the door."

"Yes, ma'am," Liam says, racing his cars all around his makeshift bed.

After helping me cover my cast, Susan helps me into the shower and washes me off the best she can while avoiding my tender spots. "That man looks at you like you're the world," she says, a smile softening her features as she helps me rinse my hair.

"How?" I croak. "And how can *I* have feelings for *him* if I still love William?" I swipe at the wetness on my cheeks. "I feel like I'm betraying my husband," I whisper

Turning off the shower, Susan hands me a towel. I take it and wrap it gently around my torso. Leaning on Susan, I hobble toward the bed and sit down.

Susan pats my leg. "You're allowed to move on," she says quietly, moving to the dresser to collect clean clothes. "William is gone. Do you really think he'd want you to spend the rest of your life alone? Do you think he'd want that for Liam?" She shakes her head. "If that man loved you half as much as you love him, he'd want you to be happy."

Thankfully, she doesn't say anything else, and helps me into the soft pajamas I wear when I'm feeling down.

Hobbling back down the hall is exhausting. I underestimated just how much energy it takes to shower, let alone doing it while trying to keep one foot out of the water. Settling back onto the couch, Susan helps prop my leg with pillows before she looks to where Liam is sitting, still absorbed in his cartoon.

"Listen, Morgan," she starts. "Sometimes, you just have to take the risk in life."

"I just don't know how I'm supposed to move on. How do I let go?" I ask.

Susan looks back to me. "I don't know," she says honestly. "But promise me you won't shut Brant out. You've been happier in the last month than I've known you to be in two whole years." She stands and grabs the empty plates. "C'mon, Liam, come help me clean up."

Liam hops up from his bed of blankets and follows Susan into the kitchen.

I'm deep in thought when the front door opens.

"I'm back," Brant says from the doorway. He's carrying a duffle bag and a pillow. "I didn't know if you had extra pillows, so I brought mine." He sets his things neatly against the wall and turns to face me for the first time. "How are you feeling?" he asks, his voice softening.

"I'm all right," I lie.

He nods. "I'll be right back. I've got something else I need to grab." He turns and walks back out the door.

Liam comes running into the living room and jumps onto the pile of blankets. "Is Mr. Brant back?" he asks.

"Yep," I say. One word answers seem to be my friend. I don't have the energy to have a full conversation. Between the pain, the medicine, and the emotional chaos, I'm spent.

"I'm going to head home since Brant is here," Susan says, giving me a gentle hug. "Remember what I said," she whispers. Standing, she grabs her purse and moves to give Liam a hug. "See ya Monday, kid," she says.

The front door opens, and Brant is trying to squeeze through carrying some metal thing, but they won't both fit through the door.

"Here, let me get the door for you," Susan says, quickly grabbing the door and holding it wide open. "I was just about to leave."

Brant steps back and pushes the metal contraption through the door first. "Thanks. I didn't want to scuff the door." Now that it's inside, I see what he's brought.

"Where on earth did you get a wheelchair?" I ask. I have crutches. What do I need a wheelchair for? I may be bruised and broken, but I refuse to be down and out any more than I have to be.

"Well," Brant says, looking at Liam. "I know a little boy who was set on being a fireman for Halloween." Liam's little head nods like one of those bobbleheads people stick on their dashboards. "I figured you wouldn't be up for trying to use the crutches around the neighborhood quite yet, so I asked around and borrowed this." He points to the wheelchair, delighted with his work. "I could have just taken him but didn't think you'd want to miss it."

Susan makes a "don't let him go" face behind his back. "That was so thoughtful, Brant. Wasn't that thoughtful, Morgan?" she asks pointedly.

Stunned, I look from Susan to the chair and back to Brant. "It was," I say, emotion making the words thick. Brant's face falls.

I hate disappointing him. It was such a nice thing to do. I can't believe he thought of a way to make Liam's fireman dreams a reality. "It really is great, Brant. Thank you."

Liam jumps up and runs to the chair. "Can I sit in it?" he asks, tugging Brant's arm. Brant nods his head, and Liam climbs up into the chair like it's a throne just for him. "This is so cool, Mommy." He fidgets and looks at all the parts and handles.

"I... Thank you. This means the world to me," I manage to finally say. Nodding her head in approval, Susan waves to the room.

"I'm going to get out of here. Morgan, let me know if you need anything."

Now that she's gone, there's an odd tension in the room. Clearing my throat, I watch Brant help Liam down from the wheelchair. "Did you eat? I think there are some slices of pizza left," I say pointing to the kitchen.

Brant nods. "I grabbed something on my way to get the chair. I figured it would be time to get this little guy ready for bed when I got back," he says, patting Liam's shoulder.

I nod. "You're right. Liam, why don't you go brush your teeth and get your pjs on?" Liam groans. "Then you can bring a book to my bed, and I'll read to you before it's time to sleep." Yipping, Liam runs down the hallway skidding as he makes the turn into the bathroom. Hearing the water come on, I smile at Brant. "Thank you, really. For everything," I say. "Would you mind helping me get to bed?"

Brant comes to the couch, and I reach for the crutches. "I've got you tonight. You look exhausted," he says, lifting me off the couch in one fluid motion. Carefully, he tucks me to his chest and walks sideways down the hallway, careful not to bump my head or feet on the walls.

It hurts to be held, but it hurts worse to try to support my weight right now. Giving in, I lay my head on Brant's shoulder. I can hear his heartbeat through his warm shirt. He smells like a mixture of soap and lemon. It's oddly comforting to be held like this. It's been so long since I let someone care for me.

Brant steps into my room and pauses. "Which side?" he asks, his voice strained. I'm sure I hurt his feelings by not being more excited about the wheelchair. Plus, who wants to spend their weekend taking care of a five-year-old and an invalid? I hate feeling like a burden. Picking my head up off his shoulder, I point to the side closest to the door. "There."

Brant nods and places me gently on the end of the bed. Reaching up, he pulls the covers down and away from the pillows. Lifting me again, he settles me in and then grabs the pillows from the other side to help prop my leg. "I'm sorry," I whisper.

Stopping with the sheets pulled halfway up, Brant's head shoots up and his eyes make contact with mine. "What? Why?" Slowly and gently, he brings the covers up to my waist making sure they are loose around my leg.

"I haven't exactly been the best company," I say. "You just seemed upset, and I— Well, I'm sorry you are giving up your weekend to be here. I know you didn't sign on to take care of me, or Liam." Tears threaten to spill again. Frustrated, I grit my teeth, refusing to cry.

"When did I seem upset?" Brant asks, confusion in his voice.

"Just now," I say. "You didn't have to carry me. I could've made it with the crutches." I'm losing the battle with the tears, so I drop my head and stare at my hands.

"Morgan," he says softly. "Morgan, look at me." Reaching under my chin, he gently lifts my face until I meet his eyes. "Holding you like that, it felt so good. When I brought you into your room, my mind went somewhere else. I'm sorry if you thought I was upset with you. Far from it."

He leans in and kisses my forehead, sending little sparks of warmth from his lips through my body. I shiver and let out a shaky breath.

"I told you, this is where I want to be," he says, stepping back as Liam runs into the room holding up his favorite book.

"I picked this one, Mommy. It's the one about the firemans and the polka dot puppy." Brant helps Liam climb into the bed. He rests his head on my shoulder, and hands me the book.

"This is perfect," I say to Liam.

Looking up, I catch Brant watching Liam with a look of amusement and love. My heart stops, and starts again so violently, it feels like it might beat out of my chest.

Maybe Susan's right, and I shouldn't close myself off.

I open the book and get lost in the words. Liam's breathing slows, and his little head gets heavy on my shoulder. Closing the book, I lift my head and blush as I realize Brant is looking right at me, his green eyes full of emotion.

"You're such a good mom. Liam's a lucky kid." He pauses, glancing away for a moment before meeting my eyes. "And William was a lucky man."

I don't know what to say. Swallowing hard, I just stare at him a moment. He lifts Liam in his arms, and slowly makes his way across the room.

"Brant," I call. "You're a great man, too," I say. Nodding, he makes his way out the door and down the hallway.

Alone in my bed, I look to the spot that William used to occupy. Reaching my hand out, I touch the warmth where Brant was sitting while I read the story. "I love you, William," I say, "but you're gone, and I'm still here. What am I supposed to do now?" I whisper.

I wake in the morning to the sound of little boy giggles and the smell of bacon. Rubbing my eyes, I wince as I shift to a sitting position. Looking to the nightstand beside the bed, I see Brant has brought in my medicine and a glass of water for me.

The slapping of bare feet on the tile hallway floor makes me smile. Liam bursts through my bedroom door grinning from ear to ear. "Mommy, guess what?" he nearly shouts. "Mr. Brant can make pancakes too! And bacon."

Brant turns the corner, balancing a tray with three plates stacked with what smells like blueberry pancakes, bacon, and maple syrup. "Liam was a big help, he knew exactly what we needed, one little internet search later, and..." He shrugs. "Pancakes. Liam, can you grab a towel so we can have a bed picnic?"

Setting the tray on the empty side of the bed, he turns and takes me in. His eyes are a caress, causing my face to feel hot. "How did you sleep?"

"All right, I guess. Thank you for leaving medicine out for me," I say, my voice husky with sleep.

Liam comes back into the room, arms heavy with towels. "I didn't know if you and Mommy needed one too, so I brought a bunch." He huffs, his little face hidden behind the stack of linens. "I had to go super slow like a sloth a'cuz I can't see." Making it to the bed, he tosses the whole stack over.

Brant grabs a towel, laughing as Liam stands proud as a peacock. "Thanks, bud." He lays the towel out at the head of the bed near me. "Hop up," he waits for Liam to get settled, and then hands him a plate filled to the edge with food.

Smiling, Liam grabs the fork stuck into the top of the pancakes like a toothpick and tucks into the pancakes, making little
happy noises with each bite.

"Do you need the bathroom before you eat?" Brant asks, a
faint blush coloring his cheeks.

"Yes, please," I say, sighing. Being dependent on someone else
isn't my style. I've had to do it all alone these last two years,
and letting someone in is harder than I thought it would be.

After helping me back into the bed, Brant takes his plate and
places it on another towel, moving the bed tray to my lap. "Do
you need anything else?" he asks.

I shake my head. "This looks perfect. It smells so good." Taking
my own fork, I dig in. For the first time in days, I am actually
hungry.

Liam is struggling into his fireman costume, and I'm listening
as Brant encourages him to work it out on his own. Finally,
Liam gets the costume on the right way and beams with pride.
"I did it, Mommy!" he says, excitement causing his voice to
rise.

Smiling, I clap my hands. "You sure did!" Sadness threatens
to sweep in and ruin the moment. William should be here
encouraging Liam.

I refuse to let anything else dampen the joy of this ex-
perience. Given the accident, I'm just happy Liam gets to go
trick-or-treating at all.

Brant helps me into the wheelchair and tucks a blanket
around my shoulders and over my legs. "You ready?" he asks.

"Yep, Liam you have to stay right with us, okay?" His excitement is already causing him to bounce from foot to foot. "No running off."

"Yes, Mommy," he says, picking up the pumpkin bucket—the same one he's used since he started toddling around the neighborhood. Apparently I'm more sentimental than I thought.

Opening the door, Brant holds it open with one foot and pushes the chair through. Liam follows outside and waits impatiently, swinging the bucket back and forth. Closing the door, Brant manages to get me turned around and down the step onto the sidewalk.

"Can we go *now?*" Liam begs.

"Let's go," Brant says, gently pushing the wheelchair along. Several blocks later, Liam's bucket is overflowing, and his excitement is starting to fade. "Mommy, my bucket is heavy," he whines. "And my feet hurt." He's already ditched the ax, having put it on my lap by the end of the first street.

"Let's head back then," I say. "You got quite the candy haul this year. Here, I can hold your bucket."

"Let's hang it from the handle here," Brant says, taking the bucket from Liam before I have a chance to take it. "What do you want for dinner?" he asks, adjusting Liam's costume hat.

"PIZZA!" Liam yells, suddenly hit with a second wind.

Shaking my head, we make our way back home with tired smiles.

After a few slices of pizza, Brant helps Liam get the shower going. "Is that too hot?" I hear him ask from the bathroom.

"Nope," Liam says.

"Great, when you're done, all you have to do is turn the knob like this, and it will turn the shower off. I'm putting your towel right here. Yell if you need me."

Coming back into the living room, Brant smiles. "That was a great night. I think he had a lot of fun. What do you think?" he asks, adjusting the pillows behind my back.

"I think so," I sigh. "I wish his dad could see him now. He'd be so proud." My voice trembles as tears prick the back of my eyes.

"I'm sure he's proud of you both," he says softly. "Want help getting settled?"

After some practice earlier in the day, I can make my way to the bathroom and back with the crutches, but I'm still very sore. Having his help would make it a lot easier.

"That would be great, thanks."

Liam snuggles in close while I read another of his favorite books. He smells like the apple shampoo he likes, and it makes me smile. "The end," I say.

"Read it again?" Liam asks, yawning.

"I think it's definitely bedtime," I say, laughing. "You've had enough excitement for one day."

He grunts. "But I'm not tired."

I smile, running my fingers through his hair. "I know it doesn't feel like it, but your body is tired. You've been a busy boy lately, don't you think?"

"I guess," he says with a small yawn. "Mommy, I don't want to go to school on Monday if you're not going."

"You need to go," I say firmly. "You can't miss school just because I have to stay home."

Crossing his little arms across his chest, his bottom lip pops out. "But you don't go to school if I can't go."

"I know, but Mrs. Susan will be there, and Mrs. Delaney will miss you if you're not there. Who will ask all the good questions?" I kiss the top of his damp head.

"Fine," he says reluctantly. "Goodnight, Mommy."

"Goodnight, sleep tight."

I watch as Liam heads off to his own room.

"I'll tuck him in. Need anything else tonight?" Brant asks, standing from where he was perched at the end of the bed.

"No, I'm good, thanks." I snuggle back into the pillows. Today was a lot, and sleep is already pulling at me.

Brant nods, flipping off the overhead light on his way out the door.

Chapter Ten

Brant

Tucking Liam in, I can't help but feel like this is right where I'm supposed to be. The last few days have been everything I've ever wanted. Doing things with Liam and Morgan makes me yearn for a family of my own.

Who knew trick-or-treating could be so fun even as an adult? Seeing Liam run to each door and wait patiently for his turn made me smile. The excitement in the air was infectious. I know Morgan feels like she is a burden, but I'd give anything to take care of her and Liam for the rest of my life.

I close my eyes and take a deep breath. An image of Morgan pregnant, and a slightly older Liam and I throwing a ball in the front yard, takes over. I want that. I want them.

Making pancakes on the weekend, trick-or-treating around the neighborhood, playing games... I want it all. Spending the last few days here has only made it that much clearer. I'm falling in love with Morgan and Liam.

Morgan has been through so much, but she shouldn't have to go through life alone. She shouldn't have to, but does she want to?

Sometimes she looks at me and I'm certain she is feeling the same things I am.

I wish I could help her see that I don't want to take William's place. He was her husband, and she loves him. I'm not jealous of that. It would be pretty crappy to be jealous of a dead man. I'd be surprised if a piece of her didn't love him for the rest of her life. That's just who she is. So loving and kind. Thinking of others before herself. It's part of what I love about her—her genuine love for those she cares about.

Taking one last look at Liam curled up asleep on his bed, I stand and slip quietly out the door.

Sunday morning, Liam and I try our hand at making omelets. Not my best work, but I think it's edible. The sound of Morgan's bedroom door clicking open sends Liam rushing to the table to pull out her chair. Good boy.

"Morning," Morgan mumbles, wiping the sleep from her eyes as she leans against the doorway. "It smells good in here."

"Thanks! Brant and I made fancy eggs." Liam giggles.

"Ready for some coffee?" I ask, already pouring her a cup.

"Yes, please, and a plate of your fancy eggs if you don't mind," she says, winking at Liam.

"Coming right up." Filling her plate, I hand it off to Liam who slowly inches his way across the kitchen and over to the table.

"This looks yummy," Morgan says when Liam places the plate carefully in front of her.

"Eat up!" He grins before racing back to the counter to get his own plate.

After a decent breakfast of omelets and fruit, we decide to spend the rest of the day watching movies together and dozing on the couch. I'd say it's just what everyone needed after the last few days.

"Bedtime, little guy," I say ruffling Liam's hair.

"Aww, but I want to stay up and watch another movie," he whines.

"You've watched a year's worth of movies the last few days. Time for bed. You have school tomorrow." Morgan holds out her arms and Liam steps into them, giving her a soft hug before heading down the hall to get ready for bed.

"I think I'm going to call it too," Morgan says, yawning. "Do you mind locking everything up?"

"Of course not," I say, squeezing her hand. "You go get some rest. I've got this."

Morgan stands and makes her way down the hallway limping and using the crutches for support.

"All right," I say, walking toward the bathroom where Liam is busy brushing his teeth. "Let's get you to bed."

Monday morning, I'm up before anyone else and make a pot of coffee. Taking a cup into Morgan's room, I sit it on the bedside table and gently adjust her blankets. "Morgan," I say softly. "Morgan, it's seven o'clock in the morning. What time does Liam need to be at school?" I should've asked last night, but I didn't think about it.

She groans, and slowly opens her eyes. "Noooo." She closes her eyes again. "It's morning already?"

Laughing, I hold out the cup of steaming hot coffee. "It is, but I come bearing gifts." I smirk as she sniffs the air and moans. "You really like coffee, don't you?"

"Yes. Coffee, yes. Mornings, no." She slides slowly up in the bed.

Handing her the cup of coffee, I lean over and pop the cap off her medicine. "Here," I say, handing her a pill. "It's time for your medicine."

She takes the pill and pops it into her mouth, washing it down with a sip of too hot coffee. "Ouch," she says, waving her hand at her mouth. "I should've blown on it." She shrugs and takes another small sip.

"What time does Liam need to be at school?" I ask again. "Do I need to walk him in?"

I've never dropped a kid off at school before. I don't know how this works, but I'm determined not to mess up.

"He has to be there at eight. You just pull up to the drop-off line and they'll take him out of the car." She takes another sip of the coffee, and her eyes close, a hum of appreciation on her lips.

The sound sends goosebumps skittering across my skin. Shifting, I try to focus on Liam.

She smiles softly. "But if you want him to be on time, you need to start waking him up now." She laughs. "He isn't a morning person either."

Shaking my head, I head down the hallway and learn for myself just how against mornings a five-year-old can be.

I get Liam to school only a few minutes late, thankfully. The teachers are just walking the kids into the building. Morgan said she'd be fine on her own for a bit, so I decide to swing by the shop.

Pulling into the parking lot, I see both bay doors are up, and cars are up on the lifts already. Daniel waves when he sees my truck pull in.

"Hey, boss man," he calls. "Didn't expect to see you here this morning." He wipes his hands on a rag and sets his tools down. "Everything okay?"

"Yeah." I sigh. "Just stopping by to make sure you guys are good. Is there a lot on the books for the day?" I ask, making my way into the small office.

"Nah, it's slow today," he says.

I nod. "Sounds about right." I look around the office, but there really isn't anything for me to do. Daniel has been doing a great job filing things away at the end of the day.

"I guess you've got this," I say, sighing. I'm not ready to go back to Morgan's and I'm not sure why.

"All right," Daniel says, taking a seat. "Spill it. What's going on?" Daniel is like a dog with a bone sometimes.

"I don't think I'm ready to go back to Morgan's yet is all," I say, sighing. May as well talk about it. "She isn't used to having someone in her space. I'm giving her time." The longer I speak, the more I start to believe myself.

"Mm-hmm," Daniel says. "So, this doesn't have anything at all to do with the fact that you'll be alone with her most of the day?" Shooting me a knowing look, he leans back in the chair and waits.

"No," I say adamantly. "Okay, maybe." I admit, hanging my head. "The last few days have been great," I say. Daniel raises an eyebrow. "Besides her being hurt, I mean."

He waits, his fingers intertwined in his lap, legs crossed like he hasn't got a care in the world.

"We've eaten dinner together, played games, and done normal family stuff." I look at Daniel. "It's been nice." I sigh. "I want that. I want that with her and Liam." Rubbing my hands down my face, I take a deep breath. "Sometimes I think she likes me too, and then other times, it seems like she isn't ready to let anyone in."

Daniel leans forward in the chair. "Then you just have to show her there's room in her life for love."

"You make it sound so simple." I huff.

"You'll figure it out," he says, smiling. Without saying anything else, he heads back into the shop and gets back to work, leaving me alone in my thoughts.

I stop at the grocery store to pick up some things for dinner. While I'm searching the aisles, I can't help but think about what Daniel said. How do I show her there's room for me too? As I make my way to the checkout, my cart filled with steaks, potatoes, and all the trimmings for a salad, I notice a display of brightly colored flowers. A bouquet of sunflowers catches my eye.

Something about the big yellow flowers makes me think of Morgan. I debate for a minute before grabbing the flowers and adding them to the cart.

I don't even know if she likes sunflowers. If not, I'll put them in a vase on the table anyway. Liam might like them. I've never second-guessed buying someone flowers before, but then again, I've never felt like this about anyone before either.

I walk through the door, arms heavy with bags, to see Morgan resting on the couch with soft music playing in the background. In her lap is a large photo album open to the middle. "Hey," she says. She glances at me, and then back to the book, softly running her fingers over the photos. I'm not close enough to see who's in them, but I'd bet my last dollar it's William.

Jealousy wars with sympathy. I don't want to be envious of him, but I can't help it right this minute. The flowers sticking out of the top of the bag now feel like the worst idea I've ever had. I move the bag behind my back, my heart sinking. She isn't ready, and she might never be. Can I handle that? I'm not sure.

"Hey," I say softly. "Have you had a nice morning?"

She nods from her place on the couch, slowly lifting her eyes from the page. "Sure," she says, her voice wobbling. She reaches up and wipes a tear from her face. "What did you get?" she asks.

I shrug. No sense in making a fool of myself now. "Just some stuff for dinner. I'll put it down and be right back," I say, shuffling awkwardly to the kitchen.

I've just finished putting the food into the refrigerator when she makes her way into the kitchen leaning heavily on the crutches. "What are those?" she says, pointing to the flowers. "Are those sunflowers?" Her big blue eyes are wet with unshed tears.

"Uh," I stammer. "Yeah. I saw them and picked them up." I am so lame. I quickly turn, looking through the cabinets to find something to put them in. "I thought Liam might like them."

"I have a vase in the cabinet above the fridge," she says quietly. "Did you know I love sunflowers?" she asks quietly.

I shake my head no, not risking my voice. Reaching up, I pick down the tall clear vase. I take the flowers and the vase to the sink. Putting water into the vase, I cut the stems of the flowers before placing them inside.

"I'm impressed you know to cut the stems," Morgan says. "I figured most men just dump them into water."

"My mom loved flowers," I say. I take the vase to the dining room table and place it in the center. "How are you feeling? Do you need any pain medicine?" I'm sure she could get it herself now that she is more comfortable on her crutches, but I need something to do so I don't spill my guts.

"No, I think I'm okay. It's mostly bearable now." She sits down at the chair I've left slightly pulled out for her since the accident. "I talked to Susan earlier." She looks at her hands. "She said she can come early and help Liam get ready for school, and she can drop him off in the afternoons. I think we can manage now if you're ready to go home."

My heart sinks. I knew this was temporary, but I thought she would want help for a few more days at least. "Uh, are you sure?" *Please say no.*

"Yep," she says looking up with a half smile. "I really appreciate all your help, but I have to get back to normal sometime." She is looking at me like she wants me to say something, but I can't get my mouth to work.

"What about your doctor's appointment tomorrow?" I ask, suddenly grasping at anything I can to stick around just a little longer.

"It's after school, so Susan is going to take me. I'm sure you have a ton of work to do this week. You don't need to be taking care of me anymore, though I appreciate you helping me for the last few days." She looks down at her lap, devoid of emotion.

Turning, I swipe all the stem pieces into the trash, and wipe down the counters. "If you're sure, I guess I'll go ahead and head out. I'm sure they need me at the shop." It's a lie. They don't need me, Daniel and Evan have it more than handled. I could probably work half days the rest of my life and they'd keep the business thriving.

"Okay, great. You can get back to work, and we'll get back to our routine," she says, her face stoic. "Thanks for all your help." She stands with the crutches. "I think I'm going to take a nap before Liam gets home. Do you want to stay for dinner?" She's already making her way down the hallway to her room.

"No, that's okay, I'll grab my stuff and leave you to it," I say, hoping my voice doesn't give away just how badly I want to stay. "Tell Liam bye for me, will you?" I manage.

She nods as she turns into her room, closing the door. The click of the latch is the sound of my hopes being dashed. Grabbing my bag and the few things I had in the bathroom, I make my way to the front door, taking one last look at the little house that has felt more like home than anywhere I've lived in my adult life.

Stopping at the front door, I notice the photo album still open on the couch. I hesitate. Part of me wants to look, but I won't. I can't bring myself to invade her privacy like that. If she wanted me to see, she would've shown me. Taking a breath, I step through the door and lock it behind me. I put the key back under the planter on the back porch and head home.

CHAPTER ELEVEN

Morgan

THE THUD OF THE truck door closing makes me jump. I finally let the tears fall when the tell-tale crunch of tires down the gravel drive fades into nothingness. Looking at my wedding photos reminded me just how fast life can change. When I caught sight of Brant standing in the doorway it hit me.

I'm falling for him, and I panicked. I can't do this again. I can't love someone again and risk having him die. Better to end things before they even begin. It won't hurt as much then.

Curling up in bed, I close my eyes and will myself to sleep. I have several hours until Liam comes home, and I can't seem to stand my own company. I drift off thinking about how nice it has felt to let someone take care of us again, even if it's only been a few short days.

The sound of the front door opening snaps me awake. Rubbing the grit from my eyes, I remind myself this is for the best. No sense in breaking everyone's hearts by getting too attached. Carefully, I swing my legs out of the bed and grab the crutches. I can hear

Susan and Liam chattering away as Liam makes his way into the house.

I slowly make my way down the hallway, the crutches banging out every forward step. I hear Liam call out for Brant and my heart squeezes. It's been just a few days, but it was as if he belonged here with us. Which is why it was time for him to go. I can't let Liam get attached to someone and then have something happen. Not again.

"Hey, buddy," I say, coming to the entryway. "Mr. Brant had to head home. Ms. Susan is going to be helping us out this week, okay?" I put on a big smile and hope Liam can't sense the hint of sadness I feel.

"Why?" Liam asks. "Doesn't he like it here?" His little face scrunched in confusion. "He said he was going to make dinner and let me help." He pouts and tosses his coat onto the ground. "I wanted to help." Liam stomps his foot in frustration.

My smile falters as I remember the bags Brant carried in earlier. "Oh, well, he dropped some things off. Let's go see what he put in the fridge," I say shooting a desperate look at Susan.

Shaking her head, she mouths, "I told you." I scowl at her and choose to ignore the niggling feeling in my gut.

Opening the fridge, I'm hit with a wave of guilt. Steaks, potatoes, and everything you'd need to make a delicious salad sit on the shelves. He bought all of this to make us dinner, and bought the flowers, and I pretty much kicked him out.

Susan peeks over my shoulder and makes a sound in the back of her throat. "Wow, that man must really like you if he was going to let you help him make steaks," she says. "Why don't you go wash up so you can have a snack and get your homework done." Liam heads down the hallway, his head hung low with disappointment.

"What happened?" Susan asks. "I thought you said Brant needed to get back to work. That's why you called me right?" A skeptical look plastered on her face tells me she knows there is more to the story.

"He couldn't stay here forever," I say, throwing my hands into the air. "I didn't know he had made plans with Liam." My face falls. It's my fault Liam is disappointed, but better to be a little disappointed now than to be crushed later, right?

"You are so stubborn. Did you even ask him if he needed to get back to work, or did you just assume and push him away?" Susan sounds mad. "I swear. You're determined to make your life miserable. Why?" Her tone softens as she searches my face.

"I am not," I say, my hands clenching by my side. "I'm protecting Liam. How would he feel if he got attached to Brant and then something happened? It would crush him," I say with more bravado than I feel.

Susan stares at me for a minute. Shaking her head, she looks down the hallway, checking to see if Liam is coming back yet. "Liam has talked about Brant nonstop since before the accident. He likes him. A lot," she says. "Who are you really worried about here? Liam, or yourself? William is gone. You deserve to be happy again. It's like a part of you died with him, and you refuse to live again." Pinning me with a stare, she turns and heads to the door. "See you in the morning, Liam. Be good for your mom!" she calls as she reaches the front door.

Her hand pauses on the handle, she takes a deep breath. "I love you, Morgan—you know that. You're my best friend. But if you think you're not already falling for Brant, you need to wake up and smell the cologne." With that, she swings open the door, and marches to her car.

Liam and I do our best to make the dinner Brant had planned. The steaks are a little burnt. It's harder to cook on crutches than I imagined it would be. Liam takes his plate to the table, and then comes back to carry mine. "Thanks, bud," I say.

Liam nods. "Where did those pretty flowers come from?" he asks, taking a bite of his food.

"Mr. Brant brought them when he dropped off the food," I say, trying to keep my voice level. The flowers were such a nice gesture, even if he didn't bring them for me specifically. They brighten up the room. I hadn't bothered with flowers on the table since before William's heart attack, and in the span of a few weeks, Brant has brought me flowers twice.

Frowning, I take a bite of my food. Did I really stop living when William died? No, right? I mean, I'm here. I'm taking care of Liam. So what if I don't really go out with friends, or buy flowers. It's not like I have time or money to do those things anyway. Who would be here for Liam? We finish our dinner in silence, both lost in thought. Liam clears the plates, and heads down the hall toward his room.

"Do you want to watch a show before bed?" I ask, not quite ready to be alone.

"No, thank you." He stops and takes a breath. Turning around, he pins me with his watery eyes. "Does Mr. Brant not like me anymore?" he asks, tears streaming down his cheeks.

"Of course he does," I say, reaching my arms out for him. "Come sit with me on the couch for a minute."

Once we are both settled, I reach over and pull Liam to me. "Mr. Brant likes you very much." I take a breath and continue. "He has to work; his shop needs him," I say, trying to take the sting out of the hurt Liam is feeling. "We'll be okay without him. We were before, remember?"

"But he said his friend was taking care of it." Liam's little body shudders. "He played with me, and took care of us," he says softly, pressing his face into my shoulder. "I miss him."

"Me too," I whisper. "Me too."

Sleep doesn't come easy for me. Susan's words, and Liam's disappointment are banging around in my head like a bass drum. I toss and turn before finally deciding I need to do something. Pulling out my phone, I decide to send a text to thank Brant for the dinner.

Thank you for the dinner stuff. I didn't realize you'd bought steaks.

I hit send and put the phone face down on the bed. If I had known Liam was looking forward to making dinner with him, would it have changed anything? Probably not. Looking at that old photo album today reminded me what it's like to be head over heels in love and lose everything. It's not something I think I could survive again.

My phone buzzes. Picking it up, I swipe open the screen, and see a reply from Brant.

You're welcome.

His short answer makes me pause. I know he said he was falling for me when I was in the hospital, but anyone might feel that way when they witness that kind of accident with a friend. There is no way he actually means it. He's still young—he can find another woman who doesn't have a boatload of baggage. A woman who might want to give him the family he said he always wanted.

That woman is not me.

A niggling of guilt eats at me, but I shake it off. I did the right thing. Liam and I are fine on our own.

For the first time in a while, I wonder if that is true.

The next week passes in a blur. The doctor cleared me to return to work on Friday, though I still can't drive, and haven't replaced my car, which is why Liam and I are rushing around Monday morning trying to be ready when Susan gets here.

A honk sounds from the driveway telling me our time is up. Huffing, I throw the apple I'm holding into my lunch bag and decide that will have to be enough. "Liam, come on, Susan is waiting for us," I shout, grabbing my bag and placing it on the knee scooter I ordered to help me get around at work. The doctor agreed it's probably safer than crutches through the hallways of an elementary school.

"I'm coming!" Liam shouts sliding around the corner in his socks. Sitting down on the floor, he slides on his superhero light-up sneakers. Flipping the velcro straps over, he stands and grabs his backpack from the hook. "Let's go!" he shouts.

"Hold the door open for me, please."

Liam holds the door, and I manage to get my scooter and my bag out to the porch. "Can you close the door for me bud?" I ask as Liam steps out behind me.

"Here," Susan says, holding out her hand. "Give me the key and I'll lock up while you get settled."

Passing her the key, I smile gratefully. "Thanks. I need to find out what happened to my car keys after the accident. This one is the spare from William's keychain."

Susan smiles sadly. "Well, add it to your list, I guess."

Once we're all in the car, Susan glances in my direction. "You all right?" she asks. "Are you sure you're ready to come back to work so soon? There's no rush. Reese has been holding down the fort, and they brought in a sub who's been helping her out."

I sigh. "Yeah, I need to get out of the house. I'm going a little stir crazy. Plus, I can't afford to take any more time off. What if Liam gets sick and I'm out of PTO?" I look out the window as she pulls out the driveway and onto the main road.

"All right, if you insist." Susan sighs. "Have you heard from him?" she asks softly.

"Nope," I say, popping the p. "Nothing since the text the night he left." I look down, picking at my nails. "I didn't expect him to contact me really, though I do need to finish paying him back for the repairs to my car. So I guess I'll see him at some point," I say, a hint of sadness in my voice that I can't hide.

"Hmm," Susan arches her brow.

Thankfully, the rest of the ride to school passes with Liam asking Susan all about why Santa doesn't bring presents for grownups. Better her than me. I chuckle before looking out the window and getting lost in my own thoughts.

I can't shake the disappointment that Brant hasn't called or texted. I'd hoped he might still come to Wednesday dinner at least. It was part of our deal, and I find both myself and Liam missing him. Turns out, sending him home did nothing to stop me from thinking about him constantly.

My first day back in the classroom is harder than I thought. I'm exhausted and hurting by the end of the day. Which is good because maybe I'll actually sleep tonight.

"I'm glad you're back," Reese says, picking the glue bottles up from the tables and placing them back into the container we keep them in. "It just wasn't the same without you."

I smile, rolling the knee scooter across the floor to put the stack of papers I'm holding into the recycle bin. "It's good to be back. I missed these kiddos, and you." I smile. Reese has really become a bright spot in my day. We work well together, and she has become a good friend.

"Ready?" Susan asks, stepping into the room a moment before Liam. "I already grabbed Liam, so you don't have to go through the whole school. I figured you'd be tired by now. Hey, Reese, girls night tomorrow at Morgan's. She needs a pick-me-up."

"I'm down," Reese says, picking up her orange-and-yellow striped boho bag. "I'll see you tomorrow," she calls, slipping out the door.

By the time we pull into my driveway, all I can think about is getting into my pajamas and going to bed. Unfortunately, that isn't an option. "Thanks for the ride, I really appreciate it," I say as Liam and I gather our things and get out of the car.

"Don't even worry about it," Susan says. "That's what friends are for. See you in the morning."

"C'mon, Liam, I'm thinking it's a pizza night."

"Yay!" Liam shouts and races for the front door. "Hey, what's this?" he yells.

I make my way onto the porch where Liam is holding something in his hands. "I don't know," I say, reaching for the package. Tearing it open, my eyes slide to the note inside. I pull out the note, and the picture book inside.

"A new book!" Liam says, "Who sended it?"

Unfolding the letter, my eyes scan for the name. "Mr. Brant," I say quietly, eyes scanning the letter. "He said he wanted you to have a new book for bedtime." Flipping the book over, I smile. It's another book about a little boy who grows up to be a fireman.

"Can we read it now?" Liam asks.

"Let's get inside and order pizza. We can read it after we eat."

Liam and I read the book three times before he finally agreed to go to sleep. Closing his door softly, I lean my head against it and release a sigh.

I messed up.

After getting ready for bed, I pick up my phone and send a text before I lose my nerve.

Thank you for the book. Liam loved it.

I wait, barely breathing, for his answer... but it doesn't come.

Tuesday passes in a flash, and before I know it, Susan, Reese and I are settled around a table full of Chinese take-out.

"So," Reese says, stabbing her sweet and sour chicken with a fork. "What is really happening with you and Brant? I thought things were going well?"

Susan drops her chopsticks to her styrofoam container, not even pretending she isn't waiting for that answer herself.

"There's nothing to tell," I say, eyeing the container of crab rangoon. "We were friends, and now we aren't." My voice cracks. Dang it. I'm not going to cry. That was the whole point in sending him away.

"Hmm," Susan says. "Seems to me there is more to it than that. Liam has walked around sad for the last week, and you're not much better."

"No offense," Reese says, "but you're miserable. You fell for him and now you're running. Why?" She reaches across the table and places her hand on mine. "I know you lost William, and I can't even imagine that kind of pain. I do know that life only gives you so many chances at happiness, and you're wasting one right now." Taking her hand back, she stabs at another piece of the fried chicken and pops it into her mouth.

"When did you get so wise?" I ask her jokingly. This conversation is making me very uncomfortable. I'm glad Liam is already in bed so he isn't hearing any of this. "I'm fine, really."

"No, you aren't fine, Morgan. You've not been fine since the day William had his heart attack," Susan says, a tear sliding down her cheek. "You deserve to be loved, and that man... that man loves you."

"I know. I know he does, and I love him too. But you know love doesn't always fix everything. Sometimes love hurts!" I yell. "Love leaves you lonely and confused. It leaves you scared and sleeping in a cold bed at night. It leaves you struggling to take care of your child, when all you ever imagined was a long life of happiness. That isn't how it works." Breathing heavy, I push back from the table and head to the bathroom.

Closing the door behind me, I let the tears flow. I love Brant, and I'm scared. A few minutes later, there is a soft knock on the door. "Morgan, I know it hurts, but love also heals. Love is goodness and light, not having to go it alone, it's making a way with someone who is there for you, always. It's companionship, laughter, and late nights staying up talking. We can't control what happens in our lives, but we can allow ourselves to be happy while we're here." Susan takes a breath. "I just want you to be happy."

A few minutes later, the front door clicks shut, and I'm alone with my thoughts. I wash my face, lock up the house, and fall into bed too exhausted to think.

The next afternoon, I debate texting him, but I'm not even sure what to say. He didn't respond to my last message thanking him for the book. I hate this awkwardness between us—we were friends.

"Hey, you okay?" Reese asks.

"Yeah," I say, moving over to the craft area. "Sorry, just a bit spacey today." I sort the markers and scissors back into the correct containers, determined to stay in the present for the rest of the day. Finally it's two-thirty and I am waving goodbye as the last kid leaves for the day. Sighing, I take a seat and stretch my back.

"Long day, huh?" Reese asks, picking up the papers the kids left behind on their rush out.

I chuckle. "Yeah," I say, rubbing my leg. "I'm not used to being unable to get around easily. I can't wait to get rid of this nonsense," I say, waving my hand over the cast and knee scooter situation.

"That's understandable. Don't worry about it. I can do the moving until you're better," Reese says, smiling at me.

I'm just about to refuse her offer when Susan sticks her head in the door holding Liam's hand. "C'mon, slow poke," she says, smiling. "Hey, Reese, how'd our girl do today?"

"Great, but I think she should take it a bit easier tomorrow." She picks up her bag and heads to the door. "Maybe you can convince her to rest, she kept spacing out all day. Though after the way our night ended, I can't say I blame her." She blows me a kiss and walks out of the classroom.

Susan looks over at me suspiciously. "Spacing out? Are you still taking pain medicine? I thought you said you had stopped that."

"I did," I say, grabbing my things. "I just have a lot on my mind today." I hope she'll take the hint and not ask any more questions.

"Mm-hmm," she says, sending me a pointed look. "Call him already."

Yeah right, and say what exactly? Nothing has changed. I still don't think I'm strong enough to risk losing my heart again.

Chapter Twelve

Brant

THE SOUND OF AIR tools and music makes its way through my closed office door. It's been three weeks since I left Morgan's house. I've written and deleted a hundred texts since she thanked me for Liam's book. She isn't ready for a relationship, and this time apart only drives home that I want it all. There isn't much I can do. I won't push her, that wouldn't be fair to either of us, or to Liam.

Shuffling the stack of paperwork in front of me again, I try to focus. I've already ordered the wrong parts once, and overbooked the shop several days in a row because I just can't keep my head straight. Daniel keeps threatening to send me home, which is funny, because I'm the boss.

I lose the battle again when my mind wanders to Liam. I hope he's helping his mom out. I miss his non-stop chatter and endless energy. I rub my hand over my aching heart. Memories of Morgan reading him goodnight stories, his head resting on her shoulder, take over. The book I left on their porch caught my eye when I was picking up some groceries, and I knew he had to have it, but I wish I could read it to him. Who knew I'd miss reading time so much?

I stopped showing up for Wednesday dinners, and she hasn't asked me to come back. In a way I'm glad. It's too hard. I can't go there and sit at the table and pretend like they aren't everything I've ever wanted in my life.

She told me to leave. I wish I'd known that morning would be the last time I'd spend time with Liam. I wouldn't have told him he could help me with dinner. I hate that I probably disappointed him.

Daniel pokes his head in my office. "Hey, boss, Evan and I are going to the Sub Shoppe, want to come with?"

I sigh and look down at the paperwork I'm not doing anyway. "Sure," I say, grabbing my jacket. "Let's go." After we close up the shop, we head over and get in the line to order our food.

The Sub Shoppe is in the small plaza next to the shop. It's the only place around to get a decent sub, and being within walking distance, we tend to order from there a lot. After placing our orders, we sit down at one of the outdoor picnic tables. The weather is nice today, a cool breeze blows through the orange and red leaves hanging precariously from the trees.

"How's it going, boss?" Evan asks. "I haven't seen you this down since your mom died." He flinches and yells, "Ouch! What was that for?" He leans down and rubs his leg.

"Don't be dumb," Daniel says, shaking his head. "Why would you bring his mom up?"

"I'm just sharing my observation," Evan says, holding his hands up in surrender.

"It's fine," I sigh. "I thought there could be more between me and Morgan, and she pushed me away. I can't make her let me in, and she isn't ready to make room in her life to love someone other than Liam's dad."

"I'm sorry, man," Daniel says, standing to grab our sandwiches when they call out our order number.

"This is why I don't plan on falling in love," Evan says, taking a bite of his sandwich. "Makes you miserable."

The rest of our lunch is quiet, each of us lost in our own thoughts. "Break's over guys," I say, standing and throwing my sub wrapper in the trash can. "I don't pay you to sit around."

Thankfully, the guys get my sarcasm and laugh it off. A few minutes later, I'm back in my office, and the sound of tools clanking in the background seeps through my closed door.

A knock on the door startles me, I look up at the clock to see it's four in the afternoon. Time flies when you're staring at paperwork, apparently. My guys don't usually knock, Daniel and Evan waltz right in regardless of what I'm doing, so it's probably a supplier or tool salesman dropping by to try and sell me stuff. The week before Thanksgiving is always full of people trying to convince me the shop needs the newest gadget on the market, and wouldn't you know it, the thing is on sale this holiday season.

A salesman is the last person I want to deal with today.

Sighing, I move the papers to the side and take the few steps to the door. "I'm not buying anything..." I say as I open the door. Shock causes my sentence to trail off.

Morgan is standing on the other side looking beautiful in a loose-fitting dress with her hair down in waves. Her leg is propped on one of those wheelie things people use to hold up their cast. She looks nervous, her arms wrapped around her middle like she is trying to stay warm, even though she has one of those long wool coats over her dress.

"Come on in." I motion for her to make herself comfortable in one of the open seats.

She hesitates a moment, and then grabs the handles and scoots inside, taking a seat in a chair across from my desk. She looks around the room, eyes going to the pictures on the walls, the tile floor, anywhere but on me. She's nervous, but why? She's the one who told me to leave.

Needing to maintain some distance so I don't just pull her into my arms and kiss her like I've been dying to do since the day I met her on the side of the road, I sit back down in my chair.

"What's up? Is everything okay?" I wonder if something happened to Liam. Her voice stops my internal questioning.

"Everything is fine." she says, sighing. "Liam misses you."

My heart squeezes in my chest. "I miss him, too." I'm not sure where she's going with this, so I decide to give her time to speak.

"*I* miss you," she finally says, looking up from under her lashes, wringing her hands in her lap.

I don't know what to say. Of course I miss her too, but what is the point of throwing myself out there, only to be brokenhearted when she leaves? She's made it clear she doesn't have room in her life for a relationship, and I don't know if I can go back to just being friends.

I guess I take too long to say anything, because she shifts to stand.

"Why did you come here today?" I ask quietly. What does she really want? I'd give her my heart on a silver platter if I thought for one minute she wanted it.

She looks at me for a long moment, like she is trying to gather her thoughts. "Thanksgiving is coming up, and Liam and I were wondering if you'd like to come to dinner." The words rush out like she is afraid she won't say them at all if she doesn't say them all at once.

I rub my hands on my pants to wipe away the wetness in my palms.

"I don't know if that's a good idea," I say finally. As soon as it's out of my mouth I regret it. I miss them. I miss having meals with them, laughing with them. If this is all she can offer me, I'll take it. Maybe this is part of the "showing her" that Daniel was talking about.

She lets out a breath and drops her head. "I get it," she says, standing. She props her leg onto the scooter and starts towards the door.

"Wait." I can't believe I'm doing this. "I'll come. Of course I'll come." I just hope I'm not breaking my own heart in the process. "What should I bring?"

Morgan glances over her shoulder, her mouth hanging slightly open as if I have surprised her. *Yeah, same.* "Uhm, how about a bottle of wine?" she says, a soft smile on her lips. "If you want to come over at ten, you can watch the parade with us." She pushes her way to the door, pausing when she gets closer, trying to angle herself to open the door.

"Sure, that sounds great." My heart is beating so hard in my chest I'm surprised she can't hear it from where she stands. Jumping up, I grab the door and hold it open for her, watching with my heart in my throat as she leaves.

"Hey, Morgan," I call. "Thank you for the invite." She nods her head and pushes away to the unfamiliar car waiting for her.

Closing the door, I rest my head on the jamb. I must be a glutton for punishment. Spending the whole day with Liam and Morgan, like a family, on Thanksgiving, is a dream come true. Too bad it's *my* dream and not hers.

The next few days pass in a blur of nerves and second-guessing. Should I go, should I cancel? Ultimately, I decide I don't want to miss this opportunity to spend more time with them. Which is how I find myself pulling into Morgan's driveway at nine fifty-five on Thanksgiving morning with a bottle of red wine and a Thanksgiving coloring book in the seat next to me.

There's an older cute red sedan in the driveway with a car seat in the back. I guess that was Morgan's car I saw the other day. Good for her. Hopefully the insurance money from her accident covered the costs.

I hope she got it checked out before making the purchase. You never know what you're getting with a used car. I make a mental note to have her bring it to the shop next week for a once-over.

Closing my truck door, I make my way across the yard, all brown and dormant, and knock on the door. I hear Liam's excited shout moments before the door swings open and he throws himself into my legs. "You came!" he says, squeezing me tighter.

"Of course I did," I say. "Why wouldn't I come?" My heart squeezes in my chest—I've missed him.

"Well, you left without saying goodbye last time, and you didn't come back." He looks down at his feet before hitting me with the saddest face I've ever seen.

"I'm sorry, buddy," I croak. "I made a mistake. Do you think you can forgive me?" I didn't realize how much Liam looked forward to seeing me. It makes my heart stop a moment, before it slams into my chest with the force of a hurricane. How could I ever stay away? If friends is all Morgan can be, I'll have to learn to live with that. "I brought you something," I say, handing him the coloring book.

"Cool! It has turkeys on it!"

"Liam, let Mr. Brant all the way in the house," Morgan says, chuckling. "You're making him stand out in the cold." Liam steps back, and I move into the house.

"It smells delicious in here," I say, handing Morgan the bottle of wine. "Can I help with anything?" Liam has already made his way back to the carpet and is getting out his crayons and settling down with the coloring book.

"No, I think I'm good for now. I just put the turkey into the oven. I'll start the rest of the food in a while." She smiles, and I swear I've never seen a more beautiful woman. I need to make her smile more. "Why don't you find the parade on TV, and I'll let the wine breathe."

I nod and head for the sofa. Grabbing the remote, I flip through the channels until I find one that airs the holiday parade. Colorful floats are lined up and big oversized balloons are bobbing up and down in the air. Marching bands and color guard teams are interspersed between elaborate floats, a huge one of which, featuring Santa, is known for completing the line-up.

Liam turns to take in the different sizes and shapes. "I want to see Santa Claus," he says. "I need to tell him about the racetrack I want for Christmas. Mommy said it's too 'spensive, but Santa has elves that build toys, so they can make it for me." He nods his head like he has just decided this.

"Well," I hesitate, "Sometimes Santa gives us what he thinks we would like better." I'm sure the accident put a damper on finances that were already tight. I'm not sure Liam's gift request is in the budget for Morgan this year, and as much as I'd love to just buy it for him, I don't think she would appreciate that.

"I need to have it though!" Liam says excitedly, turning back to the parade. "Johnny in my class has one, and he says it goes super-duper fast!"

"Well, all you can do is ask," I mutter. I don't think he hears me though; he is back to animatedly talking about each float and balloon as it passes.

I wonder if I was the same way as a boy— wanting things that were far outside the budget without realizing how much of a toll that was on my mom. Not for the first time, I think about what it would be like if Mom were still here. Would she have ever opened her heart to love again? If Morgan will let me, I'd love to help her with Liam's Christmas.

Thinking back on how stubborn she's been every other time I've tried to help her, I decide to file that away for another day. I won't ask her. Not yet anyway.

I sit back on the couch and take in Liam's excitement. I could get used to this. Heck, I want to get used to this.

"Would you like something to drink?" Morgan calls from the kitchen.

"I can grab something in a minute," I say.

"I've got it. Coke, juice, or water?" she says, popping her head around the corner.

"I'll take a soda, thanks," I say, settling back into the couch.

A few minutes later, Morgan hands me a cold soda, and settles into the oversized chair beside the couch. "How's the parade?" she asks softly.

Liam starts describing everything she missed, and I smile, taking it all in. The next hour goes by peacefully with Liam playing and watching the parade, the smell of holiday food wafting from the kitchen. It feels good.

It feels like home.

Chapter Thirteen

Morgan

THE SMELL OF ROASTING turkey and apple pie drifts throughout the house. The low murmur of the Thanksgiving parade hums from the TV. Liam is playing with his cars on the floor, his crayons and coloring book spread out beside him. He looks up every so often watching for his favorite floats, and Brant is on my couch looking the most relaxed I think I've ever seen him. A small smile plays on his lips every time Liam points at another float.

The normalcy of the moment makes my stomach flutter. I've missed this. The quiet, peaceful holiday morning. Having another adult to prepare things for and spend time with. Can I really spend the rest of my life alone? William was my everything, but even I know he wouldn't want that for me.

I tuck that thought away for later.

I'm honestly a bit surprised that Brant came. He seemed so hesitant when I stopped by the shop. I can't say I blame him. I spent days overthinking things until I finally broke down and invited him to dinner. I wasn't making any progress getting him out of my head anyway, so I stopped by the shop and asked.

All the way there, I flipped between being afraid he would turn me down, and afraid he would say yes. I've not had that much anxiety about spending time with someone since William and I started dating my senior year of high school.

If I'm being honest, I've been fighting with myself since kicking him out after my accident. I thought putting some space between us would make it easier, but I've not stopped thinking about him. I'm not sure I'm ready to be in a relationship again but pushing him away isn't working either. Ever since I saw him again at the shop, I've been wondering what it would be like to take things slow and see where this goes.

Liam adores him, and to be honest, so do I.

Brant doesn't seem like someone who's out to hurt us. If anything, he seems to genuinely enjoy spending time with both me and Liam. Having my son like him too is the extra push I need to pull myself out of my fear and put myself out there again. Now I just have to decide if the risk of losing someone I love again outweighs the risk of being alone forever.

Brant turns his head in my direction, catching me staring at him. A smile tugs at the corner of his mouth before he looks back to see what balloon Liam is talking about now.

"That one is so big! It looks like a giant turkey!" Liam's excitement always makes watching the long parade worth it.

"It *is* a giant turkey," Brant says, laughing. "I wonder who will eat that one for dinner."

"You don't eat it," Liam says with a shocked expression. "It's a balloon." He rolls his eyes like Brant should know these things already and turns back to the TV already waiting for the next big balloon to come along.

"Brant, would you like to help me in the kitchen?" I ask, standing and making my way gingerly across the floor. Thankfully I'm in a boot now and am allowed to put a little pressure on the leg. Otherwise, making a Thanksgiving feast would be extra difficult this year.

"Sure," he says, standing and pulling his arms above his head in a stretch. The hem of his shirt rises just above the waist of his jeans. A hint of muscled stomach peeks out and my insides melt like butter on a hot stove. I turn my head quickly. Hopefully he didn't catch me staring.

"What do you need help with?" Brant asks, walking into the kitchen and straight to the sink to wash up.

"Are you any good at peeling potatoes?" I hold out the bowl with the potatoes and the peeler inside.

Taking the bowl, he smiles. "Of course," he says easily. "My mom always had me help her with the potatoes." Humming, he pulls the trash can over to where he's working at the counter, and starts peeling potatoes one by one, placing them back into the bowl when he's finished.

I pull the turkey out of the oven, giving it a good baste before sliding it back in to finish off. Moving to the island, I start to prepare the brussels sprouts. Brant's humming makes me smile. Apparently, peeling potatoes isn't as bad a task as I thought. I hate doing it. The feel of the dirty skins and the slickness of the potato underneath makes me cringe a bit.

Brant helps get the rest of the food going, and heads back to the living room to watch more of the parade with Liam. The rest of the morning passes with Liam's excited announcements, Brant's humming, and the food cooking. The sounds and scents of comfort flood the house. By the time we sit down to eat, everyone is starving.

"Brant, do you want to carve the turkey for us?" I ask, handing him the knife. He looks at me for a moment, like he is trying to figure something out. Whatever it is he is looking for he must have come to a decision because he stands and moves over to the turkey.

"I'd be happy to," he says softly.

I sit and take a sip of the wine that he brought. A light red that tastes like berries, vanilla and fall. It's delicious and perfect for a Thanksgiving meal. "The wine is delicious," I say, taking another sip. "How did you know what to get?"

Brant smiles sheepishly. "I asked the guy who worked at the wine store."

I chuckle. "Good plan," I say, smiling. "It's perfect."

Once everyone has their plates filled, we dig in. Conversation flows easily, with Liam filling Brant in on everything that has happened the last few weeks. I smile as I watch them talking like this happens every day. Maybe letting Brant in wouldn't be so bad—though if I'm being honest with myself, I think he's already in.

For the first time, that thought doesn't seem as frightening as it once did.

"Everything was delectable," Brant says, patting his stomach. "I haven't eaten this good since, well, since you made me dinner last," he says, his words trailing off.

"I'm glad you liked it," I say, guilt threatening to steal the joy of the day. "Liam, can you help clear the table, please?" I stand and start collecting the dirty dishes.

"Let me help with that." Brant starts taking the leftovers off of the table and moving them to the island countertop. In no time, the table is clear, and the kitchen is back to rights.

Putting the last of the dried dishes away, I toss the damp towel onto the counter. "Can we talk?" I ask softly, my heart racing inside of my chest. I'm not sure I've ever been this nervous in my life.

"Sure," Brant says, turning to face me.

"Let's go out onto the back porch," I say, grabbing my glass of wine and topping it off. "Liam, we'll be on the porch!" I yell, opening the back door. Brant fills his glass and follows me outside. The temperature is dropping fast this time of year, but it's comfortable in the late afternoon sun.

Green patio chairs surround a round table in the center of the back porch. I sit in the seat closest to the door and wait for Brant to pick a chair. I look over to where Brant is sitting in the seat across from me, twirling his wine glass stem back and forth in his fingers.

I gather my thoughts. Best just to say it straight. "I want to say I'm sorry. I pushed you away, and I shouldn't have." I pause gathering my thoughts. "I loved William very much. I never thought I'd ever find someone else who made me want to try again." Brant looks up at me, his brown eyes searching mine. He opens his mouth like he is going to say something and closes it again.

"I'm not sure I can promise anything right now, but this time apart has only proven that you've already made your way into our lives. If you're willing to take things slow, I'm willing to be open to the possibilities." My heart pounds in my chest, sweat breaking out on the palms of my hands despite the cool weather. "I like you, Brant—a lot. I'd like to see where this goes. That is, if you're still interested." I've thought so much about whether I could give us a chance, I didn't consider he might not be on board until right this second. I feel like I could be sick.

Brant stares at me for what feels like eternity, not moving. Finally, he raises his glass to his lips and takes a long pull from the glass. "I'm good with slow," he says, pausing and looking down at his feet. "But you can't shut me out again," he says, pinning me with a hurt expression.

"I imagine this is hard for you, but I don't want to take William's place. I'd never dream of coming in and trying. He was a good husband, and a good father. I just want a chance to be a part of your life too. You and Liam both." Taking another sip of his wine, he waits for me to formulate a thought.

Butterflies erupt in my chest making it hard for me to breathe. "I don't really know what to say. I don't know how to do this, but I want to try." Brant reaches out for my hand. Grasping it, he pulls it to his lips and places a gentle kiss on the back.

"That's all I could hope for," he says gently. "We'll figure it out together."

Several minutes go by while we hold hands and drink our wine. I may not know how this will work, but it feels right to let Brant in. His thumb rubbing softly up and down the inside of my thumb is soothing.

We spend the rest of the night playing games with Liam and stealing secret glances. I haven't felt this relaxed and happy in years. I don't know what the future holds, but I'm going to try and stay in the moment and enjoy the time I have.

"All right, Liam," I say, putting the last pieces of the game away. "Time for bed."

"Do I have to?" he whines, his hands pressed together, and his puppy dog eyes on full display.

"Listen to your mom, bud. There's time to play more tomorrow," Brant says gently.

"How do I know you'll come back again?" Liam asks quietly. Brant looks to me for help. He is giving me the floor to handle this with Liam, and I am both thankful and nervous.

"He'll be around more now, Liam," I say, wiping my hands on my pants. "How would you feel if Mr. Brant and I were dating?" I hold my breath. My son is the most important person in my world. If he isn't on board, this isn't happening, no matter how much I might like Brant.

Liam looks from me to Brant with a thoughtful look on his face. "What's that mean?" he asks, confused. "Are you gonna be my dad?"

Brant chokes on the water he was drinking. "Uh." Red colors his cheeks as he locks panicked eyes onto mine.

"Dating means that we are seeing if we like each other enough to get married one day, maybe." I can feel my face reddening. "But, Liam, you know that no one will ever replace your dad, right?"

He nods. "Yeah, but Mr. Brant could become my new daddy since my old one isn't here anymore."

My heart squeezes. "Would you like that?"

Liam nods his head. "All the kids at school have daddies who come pick them up and do things together. I don't have a daddy to do things with."

Brant clears his throat. "Liam, I don't have to be your dad to be there for you. I would be happy to pick you up and do things with you." He pauses, gauging my reaction. "I don't want to replace your dad, but I'd be honored to be a dad in your life."

I wipe a stray tear from my face. I had no idea he was feeling left out. I mouth "Thank you" to Brant and reach out to hug Liam. "Still time for bed," I whisper, holding him tight.

"Kay," he says, squeezing me. "Can Mr. Brant read me my bedtime story?"

Brant smiles and holds his arms out for a hug. "I'd love to read to you tonight." Liam leans into his arms and they wrap around him, holding my boy secure and tight. Brant closes his eyes. "Why don't you just call me Brant?"

CHAPTER FOURTEEN

Brant

LIAM RUSHES DOWN THE hallway to get himself ready for bed. I risk a glance at Morgan—I'm not sure how she feels about what just happened, but I hope I didn't overstep. My heart squeezed when he said he felt left out. I remember seeing my friends rush off with their dads, talking about the fishing trips and camping trips their dads took them on. It hurt. I never once told my mom, though. I didn't want to hurt her feelings. It wasn't *her* fault my dad wasn't there.

"Did I handle that okay?" I ask, deferring to her. I don't want to rush things and scare her.

She smiles softly. "I didn't know he felt that way." She looks so sad I don't know if I should hug her or give her space.

"You're a great mom. You couldn't have known he was feeling that way." I say, reaching out to her. She puts her hands into mine and a spark skitters up my arm. Pulling her from the floor where she was sitting by the coffee table while we played, I stand and wrap my arms around her. "I never told my mom I felt left out either," I say softly.

Holding her like this is a dream come true. I place a small kiss on the top of her head. "I'd like nothing more than to be there for Liam. No matter what happens between us." I mean that too. Liam is a great kid, and I've fallen for him as much as I have his mom. "I meant what I said. I don't want to replace William, for either of you. I just hope there's room for me too."

She nods against my chest and steps back. "Thank you."

"C'mon Brant!" Liam yells from down the hallway. "It's story time!"

Laughing, we head down the hall hand in hand. Settling onto the bed next to Liam, I grab up the book he picked and smile. "You really do love firemen, don't you."

Liam rests his head on my chest, making my heart beat so hard it feels like it might burst. This. *This* is everything.

"Well, it's getting late. I'm sure you're ready to call it a night," I say as we make our way back to the living room after tucking Liam in for the night. "Is it too soon to make plans to see you again?" I really hope she says no. I don't know if I can stay away very long. Now that she's agreed to give us a chance, I want to spend all the time I can with them.

"I don't think it's too soon," she says. "I was thinking of taking Liam to the tree lighting on Saturday in downtown Piney Brook. Would you like to go?" She looks nervous. Is it because she's afraid I'll say yes, or that I might say no?

"I'd love to, if you're sure you want me along," I say. "I don't want to intrude on your plans."

"Liam would love it if you came," she says, stepping into my arms for another hug. "So would I." She says the last part so quietly, I barely hear it. A smile breaks out on my face, and my heart races in my chest.

"Then it's settled." I pull back from the hug and I'm hit with desire stronger than I've ever felt before. My eyes are drawn to her bottom lip, which she has caught between her teeth. I'd love to feel the softness of those lips on mine, but it's too soon. I said we would take it slow, and I meant it.

She licks her lips, and I groan. Taking a deep breath to steady myself, I lean in and kiss her forehead. "I'll see you soon."

It's a glorious Saturday morning. The weather is cool and crisp, and I can't wait to spend the day with Morgan and Liam. I glance over at the to-go cup tray on my passenger seat. A hot coffee, cream and sugar, for Morgan, and a hot chocolate for Liam, plus my extra-large hot coffee with an espresso shot, two creams and two sugars. I chuckle to myself, remembering they aren't morning people, and hoping the treat helps perk them up. I want today to be the first of many amazing Christmas memories for us.

Pulling into her driveway, I see Liam peeking out the window. My heart feels too big for my chest, realizing that he's been waiting for me. I give a little wave as I put the truck in park and grab the treats I brought. I can't help the smile that stretches across my face.

The door swings open as I step onto the porch. "Hi, Brant!" Liam shouts. "What is that?" he asks, pointing to the cups I'm holding.

"Well, let me in and I'll tell you." I chuckle as I make my way inside. His boundless energy would make millions if Morgan could bottle it. "Are you excited to see the tree lighting?" I move to the kitchen table and set his cup of hot chocolate down before putting Morgan's coffee down on the counter.

"Yep!" Liam eyes the cup on the table. "Is that for me?"

"It sure is, but be careful, it's probably still very hot." Liam slides into the chair and puts his hands on the side of the cup testing the temperature. It shouldn't scald him—I had them add extra milk—but you can never be too careful.

"I can blow on it."

While he makes himself busy with the hot chocolate, I look around and see dishes on the counter. "Hey, Morgan, I'm here," I call down the hallway.

"Be out in a minute," she yells from the direction of her room.

I take the opportunity to tidy the counters while we wait, washing the dishes, and setting things to rights.

"You don't have to do that." The sound of Morgan's voice pulls my attention away from the dishes. Stunned, all I can do is stare. Morgan's hair is down in soft blonde waves, the way she usually wears it, her blue eyes sparkling with amusement. The red sweater she's wearing looks soft and fits her perfectly. The bottom of the shirt hangs in different angles over her jeans, and her feet are still bare. Polished red toes peek out from under the hem of the jeans. When did toes become cute?

"You look amazing," I say, unable to take my eyes off her.

Liam breaks the spell with a loud giggle, his little legs swinging under the table as he blows on his hot chocolate.

"I brought you coffee." I point to the cup on the counter and reach for the towel to dry my hands. "Are you ready?"

Morgan takes the lid off the to-go cup and inhales deeply. "How did you know I could use another cup of coffee?" she asks, smiling. "Seriously, you really didn't have to do that."

"I know. I wanted to," I say, reaching out and giving her a hug. "I like to make you smile," I whisper. Her cheeks turn the sweetest shade of pink and I burn the image into my brain.

Several minutes later, we're all piled into Morgan's little red sedan headed downtown. The lighting won't be for a few hours, but there are vendor tables, craft stations, and food trucks to make it an all-day affair.

Morgan pulls into a parking space along one of the side roads, and Liam points out all the Christmas decorations that have gone up in the square.

"I wonder if Santa will be here," he says unbuckling his top clip and waiting anxiously for Morgan to release the bottom latch.

"I think so," says Morgan, helping him from the car. "What are you going to ask him for this year?" She smiles at me over the top of his head. He takes our hands and starts pulling us into the festivities.

"I'm going to ask him for a racetrack like my friend Johnny has. He said the cars go on their own and even go upside down! Plus, I have a really big wish this year, but it's a secret." Morgan's face falls for a moment, but she smiles quickly trying to hide her reaction.

"Liam, Santa may not be able to get you what you want this year, especially if it's a secret," she says.

Liam doesn't slow down, pulling us right to the edge of the crowd. "Yes he can. Santa can get anything," he says with deter-mination on his face. "Plus, it's not a secret from Santa." His eyes dart everywhere, eagerly taking it all in.

"All right, bud," I say. "Let's start over here and we'll make our way around. I'm sure the big man is around here somewhere."

We turn and head down the street to our right. The town has barricaded the streets around the square and popup tents and tables line both sides. Colorful wreaths and decorations are set out on tables in long rows. Several stands are selling homemade pies or chocolates, and a few jewelry stands and other DIY tables make up the majority of the booths on this side.

I smile as Morgan stops to admire the goods at each table. She lingers over a cookie plate that has a cute picture of Santa in an apron on it. "Santa's Cookies" is written in script across the top of the platter. I make a note to swing back by and grab it for her.

After several stops at the colorful tables, Liam says he's getting hungry. We move across the square to the street lined with food trucks. Liam chooses chicken strips and french fries, and Morgan and I decide to split a panini.

"I've got to run to the little boy's room," I say, pointing to the porta-potties by the entrance. "I'll be right back." Morgan nods, and I take off. I've only got a few minutes to grab that plate and drop it off at the car. Thankfully Morgan didn't bring a purse today, so I'm holding the keys in my pocket. Otherwise, I have no idea how I'd pull off the surprise.

After making my way back to the food truck, I see Liam and Morgan with their hands full of food cartons. Jogging up, I grab drinks and paper bowls from their hands, and we make our way to the tent where dining tables are set up. Thankfully we find a few seats left at one of the long tables.

"We still didn't find Santa," Liam says, his mouth pulled down in a frown. "What if he doesn't come?"

"He'll be here," I say popping one of his fries into my mouth. "I bet we'll find him after we eat our lunch." I smile and wink at him. Squeezing Morgan's hand under the table, I lean in and bump my shoulder against hers. She smiles, but it doesn't quite reach her eyes. "I bet Santa's helpers would love to help him make your wishes come true," I say more to Morgan than to Liam. I want her to know I'd love to help her this Christmas.

"Sometimes Santa's helpers have already helped enough this year," she says softly and lets go of my hand.

My smile falters. I hope she isn't shutting me out again. I know she worries about what she owes me for the tires, but I couldn't care less. With the accident and having to get a new car, the tires should be the least of her worries.

"How's your leg?" I ask, hoping to change the subject. She's been off the crutches for a while now. A removable boot has replaced the hard cast she wore after the accident. Thankfully it's her left foot, so she can still drive.

"It's okay." She leans down and rubs her calf. "I feel almost back to normal now. Physical therapy is helping. A few more weeks, and I should be feeling as good as new."

I smile. Taking her hand in mine, I raise it to my lips and kiss the top of it. "I'm glad," I say softly. I will never forget seeing her hurt. The terror I felt not knowing if they were okay washes over me again. Shaking it off, I reach over and pop a fry into my mouth. I'm not letting anything spoil our time together today.

"Morgan! Morgan Prescott, is that you?" A shrill voice calls from across the street. Morgan jerks her hand from mine. Her face turns several shades of white as the color drains from her cheeks.

"Bekka," she says standing. "How are you?" Morgan looks like she's seen a ghost. I look to Liam to see if he is also having a strange reaction to the woman, but he's happily munching on his chicken.

"Who is your friend?" Bekka asks, looking me over like I'm on display. Her perusal makes me uncomfortable, and I'm not entirely sure why. It's like she's judging me, and I am not measuring up. I've not allowed myself to feel that way in years.

I stand and offer her my hand. "Brant Anderson," I say, shaking her hand. "Nice to meet you." She looks from me to Morgan and shakes her head.

"I'm surprised to see you out with someone else so soon after William left us, Morgan," she says, her tone dripping with disapproval. "We certainly miss seeing you two at the holiday party."

Morgan's cheeks turn fire red. "Yes, well..." She hesitates, shooting me a glance. "Brant has been a great friend to me this year, and Liam enjoys spending time with him." Shame burns her cheeks. I want so badly to step in front of this nasty woman and reassure Morgan she has nothing to be ashamed of. I'm about to say something when her words settle into my chest like a lead weight.

A friend.

I work hard to keep my face from showing my hurt. I thought we had moved past "friends," but maybe she isn't ready to try after all. At the first sign of someone's unwarranted opinion, she's pulling away again. "It was nice to meet you, Bekka." I turn on my heel and, grabbing the trash from the table, I make my way to the bins set around the edge of the tent. I watch as Bekka and Morgan exchange a few more words before Ms. Opinionated waves and makes her way back across the street to the group of women she was with. Her arms moving animatedly as she, no doubt, fills them in on Morgan's "transgressions."

Morgan hangs her head a moment, then turns to find me in the crowd. Shock and sadness pinch her face. I give a little wave and wait for her and Liam to gather their things and meet me. I'm not sure what's worse—knowing that woman hurt Morgan, or the idea of this relationship ending before it even gets a chance to start.

CHAPTER FIFTEEN

Morgan

HEARING BEKKA CALL MY name was a shock. I haven't seen her since before William died. I never really liked her, but she's the wife of William's boss, so I felt obligated to be polite. Apparently politeness is something she seems comfortable letting go of, chatty gossip that she is.

Spending the morning walking around with Liam and Brant, I've felt so light and present. More engaged and alive than I have in years. I didn't even consider how it would feel to run into someone who'd known William. I certainly didn't expect anyone to be so bold as to imply I'm doing something untoward.

Hearing her judgmental tone cut into wounds just below the surface. I know I shouldn't care what people think. It's been two years. But the barb hit its mark. I wonder if everyone who knew William will feel like I'm moving on too soon. Lifting my head, I search the crowd for Brant. I see him standing along the edge of the tent with a withdrawn look on his face.

Groaning, I mentally kick myself. Of course he looks sad—I just introduced him as my friend. It's not untrue. He is my friend. But he's so much more. I almost told Bekka he was my boyfriend, but I chickened out. I'm sure she already drew her own conclusions anyway, so what was I doing? Protecting myself again? From what? Nosy women with nothing better to do with their lives than be mean to people? Ugh.

He deserves better than that. I told him I'd try, and at the first sign of discomfort, I left him hanging. I'll have to find a way to make it up to him. I help Liam gather his mess and guide him to the trash can near where Brant is standing waiting for us.

"Hey," I say, searching his eyes. "I'm sorry."

He shrugs. "It's all right," he says, dropping his eyes. "Hey, Liam, ready to go see Santa?" he asks with fake enthusiasm.

"Yeah!" Liam grabs his hand and they set off ahead of me, creating a space between us.

I follow behind them and watch as Brant laughs at Liam's antics. He's bouncing along beside Brant chattering happily. Seeing them together like this, I realize Liam has been missing out. I never considered how much a little boy would appreciate having a positive male role model in his life.

Susan and her husband, Sam, are great, but I've kept Liam all to myself these past two years, not thinking about what that would do to him. Rarely letting anyone in.

I make a vow to do better. It's not just Brant I've kept at a distance.

They quickly find the area to see Santa, not that you could miss it. They have him set up inside the gazebo. Christmas lights wrap around the top and the banisters surrounding him. Big red bows hang in a neat row around the opening. Christmas trees with beautiful colored balls hung on every branch stand on either side of the entrance.

Two women are helping manage the line. Both are dressed like giant candy canes complete with red shoes. I laugh as Brant guides Liam into the sea of people waiting in line. I stand off to the side and wait, taking it all in. I wave to Liam as he smiles broadly and bounces from foot to foot the way he does when he's super excited.

The line moves fast, and Liam is climbing into Santa's padded lap in no time. I take out my phone and snap some pictures of him smiling and gesturing wildly with his hands. I assume he's demonstrating the racetrack as his little arms loop and swish causing his whole body to wiggle. Then, Liam leans close to the fake Santa's ear and whispers something that makes the jolly man grin.

Santa sits back a second, and his finger and thumb pull at his long white beard. I can't tell if it's real or fake from this distance, but the way he runs his fingers through it makes me think it's real. He chuckles a bit and asks Liam a question. I wish I was closer so I could hear what they were discussing. How in the world do I come up with a "secret" present from Santa?

Liam points to me, a huge smile on his face, and I groan. I wonder what he's up to. Santa nods, and whispers something to Liam before posing for the photographer. Picture taken, he pats Liam on the back and passes him a candy cane before motioning for him to exit the stage to the right.

Liam hops down from Santa's lap and runs, smiling and carefree, to where Brant is standing just off to the side of the exit. Brant takes his hand, and they turn, chatting happily as they walk over to meet me.

"Did you tell him what you want?" I ask, hoping he might spill the beans on this secret.

Liam nods his head enthusiastically. "I did." He frowns a bit. "Santa said some things are for moms and dads to give. What does that mean?"

I glance back at Santa and find him looking my way with a gentle smile on his face. He winks when he catches my eye, and I blush. I wish I knew what Liam had told him. "I have no idea." Shaking my head, I point over to the section labeled *Reindeer Games.* "Want to play some games? The tree lighting is at sunset, so we have a little bit of time to finish exploring."

Liam grabs our hands and drags us across the way to the lady who's selling tickets. She's dressed like Mrs. Claus, complete with white bonnet and huge red dress. She smiles and chats with all the kids who walk through the entryway, passing out overpriced tickets to parents as they pay. At least the proceeds go to fund the local toy drive.

I glance at Brant, trying to read his mood. I wish I was as happy as Mrs. Claus here, joyfully manning the game tent. Brant has been quiet ever since the Bekka incident, and I'm starting to get anxious that maybe he's changed his mind. It's a lot to ask someone to try to be in a relationship with a single mom, let alone one who very clearly still has some issues to work through. I start to feel a bit sick at the idea that he'll want to walk away right after I've decided to let him in.

Brant smiles at me, and takes out his wallet, grabbing for the cash he has tucked inside.

"Oh no you don't," I say, pushing his hand back. "I've got this." I hand Mrs. Claus a twenty-dollar bill. Laughing, she gives us a strip of tickets and tells Liam good luck before motioning us through the entrance.

"Where do you want to go first?" I ask.

He takes a moment to look around at his options before deciding on the duck game. Handing him the tickets, I tell him to watch out for others, and set him free. The area is roped in on all sides with only one entrance and one exit. He can't go far. Thankfully, it's not too busy right now, and I can see him happily grabbing at the ducks floating by.

Brant and I walk towards where Liam is playing, making more of a mess with the water than necessary. The awkwardness is killing me. We were having a great time, and now there's a distance between us. I don't like it one bit.

"You're more than a friend," I say softly. "I'm sorry. I was caught off guard." I hope he can hear the sincerity behind my words. "I didn't know how to react to someone who knew William seeing us together. It surprised me more than anything, and... I didn't know what to say."

Brant sighs. "I know." He takes my hand and gives it a squeeze. "I won't lie and say it didn't hurt to have you pull back from me like that, but I guess I understand it." He pulls me in to his side and wraps his arms around my shoulders. "I don't know what it's like to lose a spouse, but I know how I felt when I thought I might have lost you and Liam," he whispers. "I'm sure it's not the same thing, but it was terrifying, nonetheless. I just hope you aren't second-guessing this."

Standing a bit away from the table where Liam is still happily lifting ducks trying to find the winner, I turn to look at him. "Brant, this is hard for me, but I want to try. I'm not second-guessing that," I say firmly, thankful that he seems to still be in this.

"Okay," he leans in and bumps my shoulder with his. "I'm trying too." I lean back into his embrace. It feels good to be held close to a man again, to be cared for.

Liam races from table to table only coming back for more tickets when he runs out. He's having a great time, and I'm really glad I invited Brant to come along with us. Last year I was so frazzled trying to take Liam around to the different games and waiting in line to see Santa that I couldn't enjoy it at all. It's been nice having a second set of hands.

"I'm all out of tickets," Liam says running back to us. "Can we get more?"

I laugh. "No way, that was plenty of tickets. Why don't we head over to the tree lighting area and find a spot instead?" Thankfully, Liam had spent more time in the game tent than I thought he would, and we don't have long to wait for dusk.

"Okay!" Liam steps between Brant and me grabbing our hands and leading us towards the exit. I look over at Brant, and he's wearing a smile that I'm sure matches mine.

This feels nice.

We find a spot near the back of the lawn and wait. Christmas carols are playing softly through little speakers set up at the base of the tree. People gather in groups around the green, either in chairs or sitting on blankets. I'll have to remember to bring a blanket next year. My foot is starting to ache from all the walking and standing.

The town mayor steps up to a small podium, and everyone goes quiet with anticipation. "Thank you all for coming out to our little lighting festival." He points to the tree behind him. "This wouldn't be possible without all the help from the volunteers who have worked hard to make sure this event is the best one yet." The crowd joins in applause as he lists the various groups that volunteered or donated to make today happen.

"Without further ado..." He waves his hand toward the ten-foot tree in the center of the town square. The entire tree lights up at once. Twinkle lights hang from the thick branches, and a huge star at the top shines brightly. There are large ornaments shaped like snowflakes and reindeer, and red and gold garland loops gently through the tree.

"Wow," Liam says in awe. "It's so pretty."

Brant reaches over and squeezes my hand. "It is." He says, looking at me.

My cheeks heat as I glance at him, and I look back to the tree. There's something truly magical about this time of year. I've always loved Christmas, but the last two years, it's been more about ticking off the boxes than enjoying the season.

"Can we get closer?" Liam asks, pulling at my hand impatiently. "I want to see the decorations!"

I laugh as I let Liam drag me closer to the tree. Smaller ornaments I didn't see from our spot on the lawn come into focus as we get closer. Gingerbread houses, sleds, and poinsettias all dot the greenery. It truly is a beautiful tree.

Liam walks slowly around the tree pointing out his favorite ornaments as he goes. Brant lifts him onto his shoulders so he can see the ones up towards the top. People finally drift away, and Liam lets out a huge yawn.

"Ready to head back?" Brant asks, looking up at Liam who is now rubbing his eyes.

"Brant..." Liam pauses and glances at me before continuing. "Can I stay on your shoulders while we go back to the car?"

Brant smiles and pats Liam's legs. "Feet getting tired?" he asks.

"Yeah," Liam yawns again and lays his head on the top of Brant's head.

My heart squeezes in my chest. Watching the two of them together today, I can see how much they really adore each other.

While I wish it was William here for him, I can't help but be grateful for Brant.

Chapter Sixteen

Brant

THE CAR RIDE HOME is quiet. Liam is asleep with his head leaning on the side of his car seat. Christmas music is playing quietly. A peace I didn't know I needed settles over me. "Thank you for inviting me to come today," I say quietly so I don't wake Liam.

"It was a great day." Morgan's hands are tight on the steering wheel—I wonder if she's still nervous to drive after the accident. "Thank you for being so kind to Liam. It means a lot."

"It means a lot to me too. I forgot what Christmas is like through a child's eyes." A smile tugs at my lips. "The excitement and hope."

"I just wish I knew what Liam's secret wish was," says Morgan, a hint of frustration hardening her voice. "It's bad enough I can't afford the electric racetrack, but now he has another wish I'll probably fail at too. You didn't happen to hear what he told Santa, did you?"

"No, I didn't." I reach over and place my hand on her knee. Tingles shoot up my fingers and straight to my heart. Shaking them off, I refocus. "I'd like to help. Liam is a great kid, and I know how hard things have been for you lately."

Morgan shakes her head. "I couldn't possibly let you help with that too. I have no idea when I'll be able to pay you for the tires, let alone anything else. Thank goodness for insurance, or I wouldn't have been able to get this car." She sighs.

"You don't owe me anything, Morgan. I wanted to help with the tires, and I want to help with this. Please. Let me help. Let me in." I squeeze her leg gently before pulling my hand back. "Just think about it."

We pull up to the house, the front porch light illuminating the entry. "I'll grab Liam." I say, stepping out of the car. Morgan nods and moves to unlock the front door. I carry a sleeping Liam into his room, and lay him down in his bed, thankful Morgan had him take his coat off before getting in the car seat. Removing his shoes, I pull the covers over his legs, and press a kiss to his forehead.

Stepping back, I feel Morgan behind me. "He had so much fun today," she whispers.

I smile. "So did I." I scoot out the door quietly, and step into the hallway.

"Do you want to stay a while?" Morgan asks gently, closing the door. "I might have some hot chocolate or something." She turns to face me, the dim light carrying down the hallway from the living room barely lights her features, making her look like a dream. My dream.

My hand slides behind her and pulls her towards me, my other hand reaching for her cheek. Her breath catches, and her eyes hold mine, alight with emotion. "Can I kiss you?" I ask softly, my face inches from hers.

She blinks slowly, pulling her lower lip into her mouth and biting it. "Yes," she whispers. Her soft response is all I need to hear. Closing the rest of the gap, my lips press against hers softly. A quiet moan escapes my throat. Kissing her is perfection. Like going home after a long trip. Hugging her to me, I run my tongue along the seam of her lips. Her breath hitches, and she opens her mouth to me. She tastes like cookies and peppermint. I could kiss her like this forever.

My pulse speeds up as she melts against me. My skin feels too tight for my body, and my heart is beating a rapid rhythm against my chest. This must be what heaven feels like.

Pulling back, I place another soft kiss on the corner of her mouth before stepping back. I don't want to push her too far too fast. She deserves everything. "Beautiful," I whisper, holding her to me for one last hug. "I'll see you soon?" I tear myself away from her stepping back and putting some space between us.

"You're not going to stay and have cocoa?" Confusion and desire skitter across her face.

"If I stay, I'm not going to want to leave," I say softly. "And we're not ready for that."

"You're right," she says, running her hand across my chest.

I take her hand, and pull her gently to the entryway, not quite ready to lose the heat of her touch. Sighing, I bring her hand to my lips and place a soft kiss on her palm. Letting her go, I pull my shoes onto my feet. I straighten back up and wrap my arms around her one last time, pressing a chaste kiss onto her temple. I breathe her in, imprinting this day in my mind. "Tell me I can see you again soon."

"Come to dinner Wednesday?"

I step back and open the door. "Wednesday," I say, then force my feet to carry me to my truck.

"Hey, boss," Daniel says, sticking his head into my office. "Got a minute?"

Stacking the Monday morning paperwork to the side, I nod my head. "Come on in, Daniel. What's up? How was your long weekend?"

I've always closed for Thanksgiving weekend. I know people think I'm crazy for not opening for the after-Thanksgiving madness, but I've always wanted to give my guys the time off with their families. Besides, who's getting their car worked on the day *after* Thanksgiving?

My mom always worked on the holidays, and I remember being sad and jealous when the other kids at school talked about all the time they spent with their families while I was with a babysitter. I always vowed to spend the time with my family one day, and owning my own shop means I can give that to my employees too.

Daniel moves across the room and plops down in a chair opposite my desk. "It was fantastic," he says, patting his flat stomach. "Elli and I went to my parents' house. Mom always makes way too much. How was yours?"

"Great, actually. I spent the day with Morgan and Liam." A smile pulls at my lips.

"Ah, a smile," he says, leaning forward and placing his arms on his knees. "I don't think I've ever seen you so worked up over a woman." He winks at me. "I like this happy version of you."

A bark of laughter escapes me. "I wasn't happy before?" I ask, chuckling.

"Honestly?" Daniel says, looking me in the eye. "Not really. But you're smiling more lately—well, except for the few weeks when you and Morgan weren't really talking. I like it."

Was I really that unhappy before? No. I think content is more the word. I had my business, and my friends. Well, I had Daniel and Evan. That was enough. But having Morgan and Liam in my life fills a hole I didn't realize was there. I had always wanted a family, but the older I got, the more I figured it wasn't really in the cards for me after all. Shaking my head, I wave him off. "All right, man, enough sappy stuff. What did you need?"

Daniel dives into the list of parts he needs to work on the foreign car that came in first thing this morning before standing up and heading towards the door. "I mean it, man. Morgan seems good for you. Don't mess it up." He wraps his hand on the door frame twice, and heads back out into the shop.

Shaking my head, I order the parts he needs, then dive back into the waiting paperwork. I was more distracted than I realized—what usually took me an hour or two took the entire day. Looking at the clock, I see it's already five. Thankfully I finished and I won't have to stay late. Stretching my back, I decide to pick up a pizza on the way home. No way am I cooking tonight.

Pizza in hand, I plop into the couch and take out my phone. Smiling, I send a message to Morgan.

Fake tree or real tree?

I sit my phone on the couch beside me. Remote in hand, I flip channels until I find the Monday night football game. Both teams I don't really care about, but I enjoy watching nonetheless. I grab another slice of pizza from the open box on the coffee table in front of me and settle back to watch the game.

At halftime, I reach over and grab my phone. I slide the screen open and see a missed message from Morgan. I must've left my phone on silent after leaving work. Butterflies kick into high gear, slamming into my chest when I see her name. I open her message and immediately smile.

Morgan: I love a real tree, but a fake tree is more on-budget and little kid-friendly. Plus, pre-lit means half the work is already done. You?

I smile as I type out my response.

Real tree. Though I haven't had a tree in years. Not since Mom died.

I hit send and grin like a schoolboy with his first crush when the little bubble pops up indicating she is responding. The bubble goes away and pops up several times before another message comes through.

Morgan: That's sad! Do you want to help us decorate our tree Wednesday?

My heart swells.

I'd love that.

We send a few more texts before Morgan says she is ready for bed.

Goodnight, beautiful. I'll see you Wednesday.

My fingers itch to keep texting her, but I don't. She has captured my attention, and my heart.

I glance in my rearview mirror, and for the tenth time since I stopped at the tree farm, I wonder if I'm making a mistake. It's too late now. If she doesn't like it, I'll just take it home and put it up in my own living room, I guess. I grabbed a tree stand and some decorations, too. I didn't know what Morgan would have on hand since she hinted she usually has a fake tree. I make the turn into her driveway and hold my breath. *Here goes nothing,* I mutter to myself.

Morgan said she likes real trees, so fingers crossed she likes this one. If all goes right, maybe we can pick out our real tree together next Christmas. I catch sight of the curtains fluttering back into place. Not sure if it was Liam or Morgan, but I suppose I should get out of the truck.

Stepping down, I hear the front door swing open. I reach into the bed of the truck and haul out the seven-and-a-half-foot Douglas Fir I picked up from Beckhart's Tree Farm in town.

"Look, Mommy! A real Christmas tree!" Liam shouts, doing his best impression of a jumping bean. Meanwhile, Morgan is still standing still with her mouth slightly open. Today she's wearing a pair of black yoga pants and a green oversized sweater. Black fluffy boots keep her feet warm in the cool air.

I swear she looks more amazing every time I see her.

"I passed by Beckhart's on the way to the parts store this afternoon, and I wanted to surprise you." Morgan is standing stock still. "Surprise," I say weakly. Any hopes of this being a good surprise are falling fast. Morgan still hasn't moved or said a word.

Liam runs up and touches the branches. "They are pokey," he says giggling. "Come on, Mr. Brant, we have cookies." He points to the house before breaking into a sprint and heading back inside.

"You shouldn't have gone to all the trouble." A frown tugs at the corners of Morgan's mouth, and my heart sinks. I've screwed this up.

"I overstepped. I'm sorry." Disappointment fills me. I had hoped changing up the tree might help her see that sometimes change is good. Stupid idea, really.

"No," Morgan says hesitantly. "It's a beautiful tree. Go ahead and bring it in. We'll figure it out." She takes a deep breath and rubs her hands together. "Let's get inside. We're letting the cold in."

Hefting up the tree, I follow her up to the porch, hoping I haven't messed up as bad as I think I have.

Chapter Seventeen

Morgan

WHAT IN THE WORLD am I going to do with a real tree? Shaking my head, I step into the warmth of the house. I can't decide if I'm irritated, surprised, or happy. Some combination of all three, I suppose.

"I don't have a tree stand, Brant, or lights. It was a lovely gesture, but I'm afraid we have no way to put it up." I sigh, already preparing for the fallout once Liam realizes the tree didn't follow him inside.

Brant grins. "That's all right, I've got a stand in the car, and I brought some lights just in case. I wasn't sure what you'd have since you said you usually use a pre-lit tree."

He really did think of everything. He hops off the porch and heads back to the truck, I assume to gather the other things he was nice enough to bring.

I'd wanted this to be a low-key evening. The fake tree is already standing in the corner, and it's just waiting on the ornaments to go on. Easy up, easy down. Less work for me. I'm already imagining finding the little needles all over the place and the mess I'll make dragging the tree back out of the house after the holidays. Shaking it off, I try to be grateful for the huge evergreen now resting against my house.

I do love the smell of real trees, and I did tell him I preferred them. He was just trying to be nice. Right? Why is it so hard for me to let other people do nice things?

Letting go of control is hard. It's how I've kept my balance and my feet moving forward after losing William.

Brant steps into the house with his arms laden with his load, the tree stand dangling precariously from his fingertips. Jumping into action, I reach out and grab some of the bags from his hands. "Brant, this is not just lights," I admonish. Looking at all the bags, I see he purchased just about everything from the Christmas section at the local store.

He blushes. He freaking blushes pink enough I see it on his cheeks above his neatly trimmed beard. That blush does weird things to my heart, and I find myself changing my mind about the tree. It's a sweet gesture, and he went to all this trouble to make sure we had what we needed. How can I be upset by that?

"I figured we might need extra supplies. Whatever you don't want, I can return. No biggie." He moves toward where the five-foot fake tree is standing looking pitiful now in comparison to the giant he pulled out of his truck. Setting the bags down on the floor, he turns and looks at me.

"I can take the tree to my place, if you'd rather," he says softly. "I realize I overstepped here, but I thought you guys might enjoy a real tree, and since I haven't had a tree in a few years, I wanted to treat you. I wanted to make you smile."

His plea is so genuine, it's impossible for me to tell him no. "Thanks, Brant. I haven't had a real tree since Liam was a baby. Keeping him out of it was a full-time job, and a fake one just seemed easier." I smile at him and move to grab the storage container for the fake tree. Guess that will go back into the garage now.

"Hey, wait." Brant says, mischief sparkling in his eyes. "Liam, how'd you like to have this tree in your room? I brought more than enough to decorate two trees."

Liam's eyes light up as he looks from the fake tree to me and back to Brant. "Can I?" he asks around a mouth full of cookies.

"Liam Michael Prescott, did you really get into the cookies already?" Can't let that kid out of my sight. I shake my head as he stands there, cheeks as big as a chipmunk.

"Sorry, Mommy. They smelled good, and I was hungry." Liam is busy wiping crumbs off his shirt, when Brant clears his throat, getting my attention.

"How about it, Morgan? Can the boy have a tree in his room?"

"I guess so," I say, sighing dramatically. "But Santa only puts presents under the big one." I can picture Liam now, waking up Christmas morning thinking there will be a double dose of presents under the trees. *Trees*, as in more than one. How is this my life?

Liam nods his head, and Brant laughs. "I imagine Santa wouldn't want to risk sneaking in and waking sleepy kids up. Why don't you decide where you want to put this one, Liam? I'll be right there."

Liam skips down the hallway singing a Christmas carol mashup of some sort about trees and favorite things. I can't help but laugh at his creativity.

"Are you sure this is okay? I can take it back to my house and totally take the blame on this one. I don't want to make things difficult for you." He leans forward and places his hand on my cheek. "I want to help, and I want us to have the best first Christmas I can manage. I'll even help take it down after Christmas, so you don't have to haul it out." He pauses. "And I'll vacuum up all the needles, too."

Tears prick the back of my eyes, and I swallow hard. "It's nice of you, Brant. Thank you." I lean forward and place a small kiss on the corner of his mouth. "I'm trying," I whisper.

Brant nods, grabs the old tree, and heads down the hall where Liam is still singing at the top of his lungs. Christmas is certainly going to be different this year, and for the first time in a long time, I am looking forward to it.

After we settle the Christmas tree into the stand and give it a generous amount of water, I take a step back and admire how full my living room looks. The house is already starting to smell like pine sap and Christmas past. I feel the last bits of frustration sliding off of me.

We already decorated Liam's tree with his favorite unbreakable ornaments, and a little bow I whipped together with some left-over crafting ribbon from last Christmas. I have to admit, his room looks awfully festive with the dim lights glowing. He giggled the entire time about being the only kid in his class who will have a tree in his room.

I watch as Brant skillfully adds the twinkle lights he brought to the big fir, somehow avoiding getting stabbed by branches as he goes. Liam is carefully moving behind him with the reel of multicolored bulbs, diligently following Brant's every direction with a serious look on his face. He's taking his role as helper very seriously.

The soft sound of Christmas carols floats over the little speaker on the coffee table making it feel like a normal family Christmas.

My heart swells. It might even burst from my chest. This feels *right*. It feels like home for the first time in years. I look over my shoulder at the wedding photo still hanging on my wall. William would have wanted this. For me. For us.

Once the lights are all set and twinkling away, I open the little boxes of ornaments and hand them to Liam, who places them on the tree like we do every year. Except this year, Brant is there to lift Liam up so he can reach the top of the tree too. This will probably be the most evenly decorated tree we've had since Liam started helping place the ornaments a few years ago. Usually, they're clustered around the bottom where he can reach, and all in the front so he can see them easily.

"Can I put the angel on?" Liam asks once he places the last ornament on the tree—a sleigh he made last year in school.

"Sure," I say, reaching for it. "Just be careful. And let Brant help you, all right?" I hand the angel to Liam, who sticks his arms up in the air for Brant to lift him up. After a few minutes of muttering and wiggling, the angel is up on the tree.

"It's beautiful," I whisper. It really is. The twinkling lights behind the ornaments make the tree look like it's glowing. Brant managed to get some of the lights up under the angel, making her sparkle as if she's radiating light as well.

"Yes. Beautiful," Brant says, but when I glance at him, he is staring at me.

Suddenly warm, I break eye contact and turn for the kitchen. "Who's ready for pizza and a Christmas show?"

"ME!" Liam yells sprinting into the kitchen ahead of me. If that kid ever walks, it is a miracle. "Can we watch Rudolph?" Liam asks, sliding a piece of pepperoni pizza onto a paper plate.

"You bet," I say, ruffling his hair. "Go put on your pajamas, and don't forget to grab a towel to sit on. I don't want to clean pizza sauce off the rug."

"Got it." Liam sets his plate back onto the counter and rushes down the hallway to grab a towel from the hall closet. A few minutes later, he's sitting cross-legged on the floor, his pizza on the towel in front of him, as the movie plays on the TV. Brant is sitting next to me on the couch, his knee grazing mine as he shifts, causing heat to slide up my leg and pool in my belly in the most delicious way.

I put my empty plate on the table in front of me and lean back into Brant. Laying my head on his shoulder, I sigh. Content. That's how I feel right now. And for once, it doesn't seem scary.

"Can we have cookies and cocoa now?" Liam asks, putting his plate on top of mine.

I laugh. "Didn't you already sneak cookies, mister?" I shouldn't give him anymore, but it's Christmas. I stand and grab the plates, taking Brant's with me as I go. "Coffee or cocoa?" I ask him.

"Cocoa," he says, smiling. "Would you like help?" Standing, he follows me into the kitchen.

"If you want. You can take the plate of cookies out to the living room," I say, putting the kettle on the stove to warm. I turn and find Brant standing so close to me I can feel the heat radiating off of his body.

"I've wanted to do this all night," he whispers, leaning in and placing a soft kiss on my mouth. Warmth spreads from our joined lips through my entire body. I want more. Leaning in, I press myself closer to him and wrap my arms around his neck.

He groans and deepens the kiss, pressing me back against the countertop with his hands on my hips. I kiss him back, losing myself in his kisses. I don't know how much time has passed, but I know I wasn't ready to stop kissing him.

The kettle starts to whistle, breaking the spell. He leans his forehead against mine as we both try to catch our breath. Reaching behind me, he flips the burner off, grabs the plate of cookies, and winks before heading into the living room.

"Cookies!" I hear Liam yell.

"Just one!" I shout. I press my hand to my chest and let out an unsteady breath. My heart pounds in my chest. I forgot what it's like to be kissed like you're the only thing that matters. I touch my swollen lips, the tingle a reminder of his lips on mine.

I grab three mugs, quickly mix the hot cocoa packets in and drop a few marshmallows on top for good measure. I put extra milk in Liam's cup so it's cool enough for him to drink right away. I grasp the handles of all three mugs and carefully make my way to the living room. Sinking into the couch next to Brant, I blow across the hot cocoa in the reindeer-shaped mug in my hand.

I should've gotten ice water. I'm still hot and bothered by that kiss.

Brant reaches over and links his free hand through mine. We sit, sipping hot cocoa and holding hands until the movie finishes and the last credits have rolled, neither one of us ready to break the spell.

CHAPTER EIGHTEEN

Brant

I LACE MY FINGERS through Morgan's and hold our hands on my thigh. It feels wonderful to hold her like this. I was worried about the tree, but it seems like it worked out in the end. It looks wonderful in her living room and makes the space feel like Christmas to me.

We didn't have much growing up, but Christmas was special. It was the time of year that we always spent time watching classic movies, baking cookies, and enjoying time together, as much as Mom's schedule would allow.

Every year, we'd make hot chocolate, bundle up, and drive around looking at Christmas lights. It was the highlight of the year for me, and we continued to do it until Mom passed away. I didn't realize how much I've missed the festivities of the season. I'll have to take Liam and Morgan to look at lights this year.

The movie ends, and Liam is passed out on the floor by the tree. "Do you want me to carry him to his room?" I ask softly, not wanting to wake him.

"That would be great." Morgan stands and stretches her arms above her head bearing the slightest bit of stomach. Just enough to make my pulse kick up and my mouth run dry. She really is the most beautiful woman I've ever seen. That kiss in the kitchen was mind-blowing. Thank goodness for a screeching kettle, or I might have embarrassed myself.

Morgan tiptoes down the hallway to get his bed ready, and I make my way over to where Liam is asleep on the floor. His face is lit by the glow of the tree, and he looks like a sleeping angel. I stand there, soaking him in for a minute before bending down. I scoop him into my arms, and he nuzzles his head into my chest. I smile. I think I understand how the Grinch must have felt when his heart grew three sizes. Gently I hold him to me and walk him carefully into his room. Laying him on the bed, I press a kiss to his forehead and step back. Morgan pulls the blankets up over him and gives him a kiss of her own.

We quietly make our way out of his room and close the door. "Thank you," Morgan whispers.

I take her hand and lead her back into the living room where the tree is still twinkling softly. "Don't forget to turn that off before you go to bed, and check the water every other day," I remind her. "We don't want any accidents."

I lean in and kiss her softly on the lips. Pulling back slowly, I'm captured by her beautiful eyes. "You really are the most beautiful woman I've ever known," I say before leaning in to kiss her again.

Morgan wraps her arms around my neck and pulls me closer, deepening the kiss. Reluctantly, I pull back. "Stay a while longer?" Morgan asks softly, her eyes not quite meeting mine. "We can watch another movie."

I hesitate. I'd like nothing more than to stay right here and never leave. But I've waited a long time to feel this way about someone, and I'm not going to mess it up by rushing. I kiss her again softly and pull away. "I need you to know, I want nothing more than to stay here with you," I say, holding her face in my hands. "But I don't want to hurry this—we're just finding our way. I care about you, Morgan, and Liam too. I know what I want; I want it all. In time."

She nods and leans into my hands. "Thank you for giving me time," she says softly.

"I know this is hard. We'll get there, Morgan. I don't want to mess this up by rushing things." I kiss her one more time, then gather my things and head to the truck. Leaving is the right thing to do, but it takes everything I have to follow through.

Friday morning, I wake with the chills and a headache. I haven't felt this bad in a long time. Throwing back the covers, I push to sit up and slide my feet off the side of my king-size bed. A wave of dizziness hits me. Crap. I reach out and steady myself with the headboard.

I feel around for my phone on the bedside table and punch in Daniel's number. After a few rings, he picks up, practically yelling in my ear. Pulling the phone back a few inches, I manage to get out a gruff hello.

"Brant, is that you? You sound weird—are you okay?" Daniel is still screaming into the phone. Doesn't this man know how early it is?

"Can you stop yelling?" I whisper. "I'm pretty sure I'm sick." I groan as I'm hit with another round of chills. "I'll be out today." Hopefully I'll be better by Monday. I hate missing too much work. They may not need me, but it's still my shop.

"I've got this boss. Do you need anything?" It doesn't escape my attention that Daniel is someone I can always count on. I need to give the man a raise.

Later. Right now I need to find some cold medicine and get back into bed.

"Nah, I think I'm all right." I shiver, pushing to my feet to find that medicine. "I'm just going to sleep it off."

"All right, let me know if you need me to stop by after work with anything," he offers.

"Will do," I say before hanging up and throwing my phone back onto the nightstand.

I head to the kitchen for a glass of water and hope I find some medicine.

Digging around in the cabinet where I keep the first aid supplies, I finally find a box of cold medicine. I flip it over and find the box hasn't even expired yet. Score one for me. Pulling the packet out, I tear off one of the little squares. Opening the blister packet, I throw the pills into my mouth and down them with the water. Refilling the glass, I head back to bed, and wait for the shaking to stop.

It's getting dark when I hear a knock at the door. Shoot. I hope Daniel didn't come by here anyway. Pulling the blanket off the bed and wrapping myself in it, I head to the front door. The medicine must have really helped, I seem to have slept all day.

Pulling the door open, I brace myself for the blast of cold from outside. "Hey, sorry. I didn't need any— Oh," I stutter. "I thought it was Daniel. I'm sorry." Morgan is standing on my porch with a pot of something that smells suspiciously like chicken noodle soup.

"Can I come in?" she asks, lifting the heavy pot a bit.

"I wouldn't if I were you." I groan. "I've not felt this bad in years." Just as I'm about to tell her thank you, I'm hit with another bout of chills that make my teeth chatter. "I think I have the flu or something." I groan and pull the blanket tighter around my shoulders.

Morgan pushes past me and puts the soup on the counter. "Your home is beautiful," she says, looking around a moment. "Close that door."

Shocked that she pushed past me and is in my house, it takes me a minute before I realize I'm only letting the cold air in. I close the door. I'm still standing in the entryway, staring at her across the room. The open floor plan of my house means the kitchen, dining, and living rooms are all one big space. She marches towards me as I back into the wall. "Seriously, Morgan, I'm sick. You shouldn't get near me."

Shaking her head, she looks at me a moment before placing her hand on my forehead. "You're burning up," she scolds. "Where is your thermometer?"

"Thermometer?" I repeat. "Uhm, I don't have one," I say sheepishly. "I haven't been sick in forever, and well, I just don't ever think about getting one until I'm too sick to go out."

She makes a tsking sound and points to the couch. "Sit," she orders, and turns to take off her hat and gloves. She hangs her coat on the hooks attached to the wall beside the door and tucks the gloves into the pockets.

I make my way over and plop down onto the brown leather sofa. Standing is taking too much energy anyway. "Where is Liam, and how did you know I was sick?" I ask.

She's moving around the kitchen opening and closing the cherry cabinets like a woman on a mission. "I stopped by the shop to surprise you, and Daniel told me you'd called in sick. Liam is sleeping over at Susan's tonight." The clatter of dishes lets me know she found the bowls.

"Oh," I say, nodding my head. It takes a minute, but her words finally penetrate my fevered daze. "Wait, what?" I ask, stunned. "Why is Liam at Susan's?" Morgan hardly ever lets Liam out of her sight, let alone sleep over. Even at Susan's.

"Because," Morgan says, drawing out the word. "I was planning to surprise you with a date night all to ourselves." She comes into the living room and hands me a bowl filled with the most amazing-smelling soup.

"Is this homemade chicken noodle soup?" I ask stupidly, looking at the big chunks of chicken, diced carrots and celery, and thin noodles.

"It is." She hands me a blister packet with medicine in it. "Take these and eat the soup." She sits down on the other end of the sofa and smiles softly. "I'm sorry you're not feeling well."

After taking the medicine, I breathe in the heavenly scent of chicken broth, garlic, and carrots. It smells amazing. "Aren't you afraid of getting sick?" I ask as I bring a spoonful of soup to my mouth.

"You're forgetting, I'm a teacher. I'm around germs all the time." She smiles softly. "Besides, you obviously need someone to take care of you."

My chest warms, whether it's the soup or her words I'm not sure, but it feels good. I've not had anyone take care of me since I was a teenager. By the time I was an adult I was taking care of Mom, I didn't want her to burden herself with me anymore than she already had.

"Thank you," I say, my voice thick with emotion and gratitude.

I take slow bites of the soup, trying not to splash any on myself. Morgan was planning a special night for us. I wonder if she has any idea how much that means to me.

Leaving her house Wednesday night was hard. I may not want to move too fast, but I can't help the way she affects me. I'd love nothing more than to spend every single day with her and Liam by my side.

I peek at her over the top of the bowl. Her cheeks are flushed from the cold, making them the barest shade of pink. Her hair is pulled back into a messy bun, and she's ditched her work clothes for a pair of gray sweatpants and a sweater that has the leg lamp from her favorite Christmas movie on it.

She is adorable.

The medicine seems to be helping. The shaking has finally stopped, thank goodness. I feel awful her plans for us got messed up, but I'm excited that she's open to spending time alone. I love Liam, but it would be nice to spend some time with just the two of us as well.

Chapter Nineteen

Morgan

Brant looks miserable wrapped in his comforter sipping soup off the spoon like a little kid. I'm glad I decided to visit. I take another look around his house. The living room is big with a comfy brown leather sofa and matching loveseat. There is a fireplace in the corner that looks like it's rarely used, and a big screen TV set atop a cherry wood cabinet across from the couch.

The kitchen is beautiful, with beige and brown granite counter-tops and cherry wood cabinetry. The sink is one of those farmhouse sinks I always dreamed of having. Off to the side of the kitchen is a small dining table with four chairs. It looks like it's rarely used. The walls are painted a very soft tan, and mostly bare. A few photos of what looks like his mom grace the mantle.

"I am not much of a decorator," he mumbles, noticing me look around. "I never know what would look good, so I just skip it."

I stand and grab his empty bowl. "Your home is beautiful. I don't know what I expected, really—I guess a bachelor pad with a mess everywhere—but it's so neat." I put the bowl into the dishwasher and wipe up the counter where I spilled a bit. "I love it."

Instantly I feel badly about having him over to my little house with the closed-off rooms and old peeling wallpaper. It's an older house, but it was perfect for our growing family when we bought it. We never could have afforded something as nice as Brant's place.

I store the rest of the soup in the fridge for him to heat up later, and head back into the living room. Brant is leaning against the back of the couch with his eyes closed, his breathing even and slow. The medicine must have kicked in.

Smiling to myself, I nudge him gently. "Brant, you probably want to go get into bed." He grunts and shifts sideways onto the couch. Laughing softly, I press my hand to his head. It's cooler now than when I got here. Thank goodness.

I wash my hands in the kitchen before grabbing more medicine and another glass of water. I place both on the coffee table and dig in my purse to find a piece of paper and a pen.

I leave a little note so he knows I've gone.

I grab my things and close up the house behind me. Hopefully he sleeps through the night and feels better tomorrow.

Not quite ready to head home, I drive through the neighborhood and take in the Christmas decorations. I'm rarely without Liam, and I'm never really sure what to do with myself when he's gone. I decide to stop by the store and do a little shopping since I'm kid-free.

Walking into the store makes my eyes ache. Bright florescent lights, too-loud Christmas music, and people everywhere does not sound like my idea of a good time. I'd much rather be at Brant's right now, wrapped up in his arms. Poor guy—he really did look awful.

I make my way to the toy aisle and scope out the electric racetracks. I cringe when I see the price tags. Thankfully, we've never done quantity over quality with presents, so he'll be more than happy with the racetrack and maybe one or two small things.

I pop it into the cart and keep moving. I add a container of slime —yuck— and a new game to the buggy. It's not much, but it will have to do.

Pushing the cart back toward the front of the store, I pass by a display of family Christmas pajamas. I've always wanted to dress in the same P.J.'s and take a family picture on Christmas morning.

Grabbing a set for Liam, I start looking for the matching set in the women's bin. Nope. All gone. I dig through the men's bin looking for a men's medium. That would work. My eyes land on a set of extra-large, and my mind jumps to Brant. Would he want to dress up with us? Before I can talk myself out of it, I've thrown a medium and extra-large into the cart as well.

I make it all the way to the check-out line before I'm hit with second thoughts. Taking both sets of the adult PJs out of the cart, I let the cashier know I don't want them after all, and I check out.

I spend the rest of the night overthinking and freaking out. I should've just gone and gotten Liam last night.

Being alone gives me too much time to think.

"He was so sick," I say to Susan over the cup of coffee she handed me. "You should have seen his house." I take a sip of the too hot coffee and gather my thoughts. "It was so much nicer than anything I've even dreamt of."

Susan scoffs. "It's a house, honey, not a castle." She is picking at the scone I brought with me this morning from the bakery down the street.

"Yeah," I sigh. "But it is a clear reminder that we're in two very different worlds. Why would a man who owns his own business and a beautiful house want to deal with a widowed single mother who's broke and barely keeping it together?" I pick an orange scone out of the box and place it on the plate in front of me.

"What are you talking about?" Susan asks incredulously. "That man would have to be stupid or blind not to see how amazing you are. You and Liam both. You're a catch, and don't you doubt it."

"You're a good friend," I say laughing at her outburst. "But he doesn't have kids of his own. What if one day he decides he wants kids? I don't know if that's something I want to do again." My brain has been spinning in circles ever since I left Brant sleeping on his couch last night. "I just don't think I can be what he deserves."

And that is really the heart of it, isn't it? He deserves to be loved fully and not live in the shadow of someone's previous marriage. He should marry and have kids and live life in his beautiful house with his beautiful wife and their beautiful kids.

Susan holds out a napkin. "Why are you crying?" she asks softly. "You don't have to have every single thing planned out ahead of time, you know." She shakes her head. "Did I ever tell you that Sam and I tried having kids for several years when we were first married?"

Wiping my eyes, I shake my head. I always assumed they were waiting. I had no idea they had tried and it hadn't happened for them.

"We married young, barely out of high school. We knew what we wanted though. I would be a teacher, and he would be an accountant. We would get pregnant right away and I'd finish school because our moms would love to watch the baby while I was in classes." She sighs and looks at her hands. "I had two miscarriages, and then nothing."

I'm not even sure what to say. Reaching out, I place my hand on hers. "I'm sorry," I whisper. "I had no idea."

"It turns out it's hard for me to get pregnant because I don't really ovulate much. My hormones are a mess." She looks up at me, tears swimming in her eyes. "I was sure that Sam would be better off without me. I even tried to serve him divorce papers." She laughs and shakes her head.

"What happened?" I ask, stunned.

"He tore them up right in front of me. Said he didn't care if we never had a kid of our own, that he loved me for me, and I was all he needed." A small smile crosses her face as she wipes a tear that broke free. "I kept waiting for him to change his mind, and he still hasn't."

She looks over at me and takes my hands in hers. "Sometimes we think we have it all planned out, but life doesn't follow our plans. If it did, I'd have a house full of babies, and William would still be here with you."

I try to pull my hands from hers, but she holds on.

"I'm not saying you shouldn't consider these things, but I am saying that you shouldn't assume you know what is best for Brant. He is a grown man, and capable of giving his heart to whomever he wants, with intention and thought."

I hear what she is saying, but I don't think it's that easy. I have a lot of baggage and a son to take care of. It's not simple.

"Give him a chance to decide for himself," she says with a final squeeze to my hands. I nod, not entirely sure if I'm agreeing with her, or trying to make her feel better.

Sunday morning, Liam is busy gathering the ingredients for pancakes when my phone rings. My heart lurches in my chest.

Sure enough, it's Brant. I hesitate before swiping to answer the
call.

"Hello?" Brant's deep voice asks after a moment of silence.

Clearing my throat, I try to sound normal even though my heart
is skipping around in my chest. "Hey." There, I did it. I got a word
out. Not so hard.

"Hey," he says, sounding a whole lot better than when I saw him
Friday evening. "Thanks again for the soup. That was really nice of
you."

"Oh," I stammer. "You're welcome, no problem. What are friends
for, right?" Even as it comes out of my mouth I cringe. It tastes bad
in my mouth. Friends.

"Morgan," Brant says, his voice dropping low. "Friends? I thought
we were a bit more than that. What's going on?" He sounds hurt.

Shoot. This is why I can't do this kind of stuff. Someone is going
to get hurt, and I have a feeling that someone is going to be me. I
glance over at Liam who is happily banging around in the cabinets
looking for the bowl we use to mix the batter. This is going to hurt,
and Liam is going to be so upset that I'm breaking my promise.

"I'm sorry," I whisper. "I don't think this is going to work." I hang
up before he can say anything that might change my mind.

I can't let Liam get attached and then have Brant decide he
should have had his own kids. I can't get attached and then
have him decide he needs more than I can give. I'm just not that
woman. Susan's situation is different. They were already in love
and married. What I feel for Brant isn't love, or at least it's not

the same thing I felt for William. My love for William was all consuming, with Brant, I feel light, content, happy. That isn't love is it? Then why am I standing here with my chest cracked wide open?

CHAPTER TWENTY

Brant

WHAT THE HECK JUST happened? In the span of forty-eight hours, she went from wanting to take care of me, to not being able to do this? The minute the words were out of her mouth I wanted her to take them back. My heart shattered in my chest, shards of brokenness slicing and tearing through my chest.

I sit staring at the phone for who knows how long. I know she's scared. Heck, I'm scared too. I've never felt this way about anyone before. My heart belongs to her, and to Liam. There isn't anyone else I would rather be with.

Determined, I make my way into my room to shower and change. This conversation isn't over yet. And the next time she tells me she can't do this, it will have to be to my face.

It's after two o'clock when I pull into her driveway. Liam is playing in the yard, bundled from head to toe against the cold. It doesn't usually snow here, but it's almost cold enough this year. I wouldn't be surprised to see flurries soon.

I step out of the truck just as Liam jumps up from his spot on the grass. He stands there looking at me with a scowl on his face. Uh oh. "Hey Liam, what's up little man?" I ask, trying to keep the mood light.

He crosses his little arms over his chest and stomps his foot. "You made Mommy cry." He accuses. I made Morgan cry? My heart sinks. What did I say before I fell asleep on the couch? I rack my brain trying to think of anything that would have caused this kind of fall-out, but I come up empty.

"I'm sorry, Liam." I say genuinely. "I don't know what I did, but I'm here to try to make it better, okay?" I wait for him to say something. Having his approval means everything to me. If he doesn't want me seeing his mom, I'll back off. He may be little, but he was here first.

He stares at me for what feels like an eternity before turning and walking to the front door. Opening the door, he turns back and says, "Come on." My feet move before my brain can catch up. "Mom," Liam calls from the doorway. "Someone is here."

I can hear Morgan moving around in the kitchen before the sound of the refrigerator door closing echoes through the house. I glance over at the tree and my heart swells. That was a perfect night, and I want more. I want a lifetime of perfect nights.

A gasp tells me Morgan knows I'm here. I turn and look at her. She has dark circles under her red eyes. She has been crying—Liam was right. "What are you doing here?" she asks, wrapping her arms around herself.

"I'm going back outside." Liam turns and closes the door behind him. He may only be five, but he's a smart kid.

I had so many questions and things I was going to say, but seeing her like this, I just want to hold her. My arms reach for her instinctively, before dropping back to my side. "I don't understand,"

I say, trying to hide how much pain I'm in right now. "I thought you were in this. *We* were in this. What happened?"

I wait for an answer, but nothing comes. Morgan stares at her feet, still holding herself together.

"Morgan, talk to me. Friday you came and brought me soup and took care of me. I never felt so cared for in all my life. Then today you tell me you can't do this. So I'm asking you again, what happened?"

She takes a breath before looking me in the eyes. "You deserve more than this!" she yells, throwing her hands out. "I'm a mess. My house is small, and in need of repairs. I am a widow who will never stop loving her first husband. I have a son who will always be my priority. There are more days in the month than dollars in the bank. I barely scraped enough together to buy my son a racetrack for Christmas."

She takes a breath and continues. "You deserve a woman who doesn't hold you back. Someone who can give you babies of your own, someone who can love you without a piece of her belonging to someone else." A sob breaks from her chest and she sinks onto the couch. "Please, just go."

In three strides I'm across the room in front of her. Dropping to my knees, I look at her. "Morgan, look at me." She shakes her head. "Morgan," I say softly, stroking her hair with my fingers. "You are a woman who loves completely. You loved William, and he loved you. I would never expect you to stop caring for him."

She lifts her sad face to me, and I wipe the tears from her eyes. "You are everything I have ever wanted. You are smart, kind, loving, and the best mom I have ever met. I would love to have more babies with you, but I understand if that isn't something you want. I don't need more children, Morgan. I love Liam like he is my own."

She whimpers but doesn't pull away from me.

"I don't care about the size of your house, or repairs. I'll fix things all day long if it means spending time with you. I care about you. I care about Liam. The last few months have been the best months of my life. I wasn't kidding when I told you that you're it for me. I've dated enough to know I don't want anyone else." I pull her into my chest and wrap my arms around her holding her close. "Do you think I haven't thought about your love for William? Or the fact that you may not want more kids?" She shrugs her shoulders. "I've considered all of those things, and do you know what I decided?"

Leaning back, she shakes her head and wipes her eyes, bracing herself for whatever I say next. "I love you, Morgan. I love you and Liam more than I ever thought I could love anyone in my life. If you never want to have another baby, I'm good with that. Liam is an amazing kid and I'd be happy to be a part of his life."

She finally looks up at me.

"If you wanted ten more babies, I'd do my best to give them to you." I wink and smile. "I know you will always love William, and to be honest, that's part of what I love about you. You love so big and so hard, that once you let someone in, they're always in." I lean in and kiss her temple. "Let me in," I whisper.

My heart stops beating while I wait for her to say something. Anything. "Okay." She leans her head into my chest.

"Okay?" I ask. I have to be sure I heard her right. She nods against my chest. I hug her tight to me. My heart feels like it is beating a million times a minute. I kiss the top of her head. "I love you," I whisper. "You don't have to say it back, but I need you to know how I feel. I love you, and I love Liam. I always will."

She wraps her arms around me and leans her head back, looking into my eyes. "I love you too, Brant."

I close my eyes absorbing those three little words. "Grab your coat—there is something I want to show you." I stand and help her to her feet. She hesitates for a moment, looking unsure. I lean in and kiss her. "Trust me."

Stepping outside, I head over to Liam. "Hey, bud, you want to go for a ride? I've got something I'd like to show you and your mom."

He pins me with his chocolate brown eyes. "Is Mommy still sad?"

I shake my head no, and his face lights up. I'm ready for it this time when he slams his little body into my legs. Snagging him up, I hug him tight. "I'm sorry your mom was sad. I don't like it when she's sad either." I wait for him to nod before I continue. "I want to spend the rest of my life making you and your mom happy, little man."

Liam throws his arms around my neck and squeezes tight. "Let's go," he yells as his mom steps out the door. Morgan settles Liam into the back of her car, and I hold out my hand.

"Keys please," I say. Morgan smiles and drops the keys into my hand before hopping into the passenger seat.

I'm more nervous now than I think I've ever been in my life. This could be wonderful, or it could set us back again. Hopefully, it proves that I understand her. I head in the direction of the surprise and hope she doesn't catch on too soon.

By the time I take the last turn, I'm holding my breath. Morgan is looking at me from the other side of the car, her beautiful face scrunched in confusion.

I pull up to the spot I'm looking for and put the car in park. Reaching over, I take Morgan's hand and bring it to my lips. "William will always be a part of your life, Morgan. He is always going to be your first love, and Liam's dad. I respect that. I'm sorry he isn't here anymore for you two," I say. "But I'm *not* sorry that I get to be the man who loves you and Liam now."

I turn and hop out of the car. I unbuckle Liam and take his hand as he steps out. Morgan is already standing on the other side of the car looking out over the field in front of us. Moving to her, I take her hand in mine, and together the three of us head to William's grave.

I stopped by earlier to visit my mom's grave and made a decision to have a heart-to-heart with one William Prescott. Before I left, I arranged a wreath at his headstone and cleared the leaves out of the way.

"We'll always make sure William is a part of our life. Liam won't forget who he is, because we won't let him," I say, squeezing Morgan's hand. Liam moves to touch the wreath laid against the headstone and smiles.

"It's Christmas for Daddy, too," he says softly.

Morgan nods, tears streaming down her face.

"I'll give you two some time." I turn and make my way back to the car. Climbing inside, I watch them stand together and talk.

After a while, Morgan and Liam touch the headstone and return back to the car. Once everyone is buckled back up, she faces me and smiles. "Thank you," she says softly, taking my hand.

"You're welcome."

"Do you think we can see my daddy again soon?" Liam asks from the back seat.

I smile softly and turn so he can see my face. "Absolutely," I say. "Anytime you want to come see your daddy, I'll be happy to bring you."

Liam nods and looks out the window to his dad's site again. "'Kay," he says softly.

The sun is setting behind the clouds by the time we are heading back home, and I'm struck with another plan. "Who wants hot cocoa?" I ask, turning the car into the coffee shop parking lot. "I think it's the perfect night for hot cocoa and donuts for dinner. What do you think?" I ask, smiling at Morgan.

She laughs as Liam shouts his enthusiastic yes from the back seat. "You're too much sometimes," she says chuckling. "Good thing I love you."

We grab an assortment of donuts and hot cocoa with whipped cream for dinner. Taking them to-go, I help Liam back into his seat before handing him his cocoa and a donut wrapped in a napkin.

"Ready, bud?" I ask, excitement nipping at me.

"Yep," he says, taking a huge bite of donut and smiling. I laugh and slide into the driver's seat.

Morgan is blowing onto her hot cocoa, donut balanced on her leg. "This is crazy," she says, humor lighting her eyes. "Now what?" she asks.

Laughing, I lean in to kiss her temple. "We go look at Christmas lights," I whisper.

Turns out, looking at Christmas lights isn't my favorite part of the holidays anymore. It's spending it with these two.

Epilogue

CHRISTMAS MORNING

I PAD DOWN THE hallway quietly, grateful that Liam isn't a morning person. Opening the door, I shiver as cold air blows the bottom of my robe open. "Come in, quick," I whisper, opening the door a bit wider. Brant steps in and quietly clicks the door closed, shutting out the cold air. "Merry Christmas," I say, leaning in to wrap him in a hug.

"Merry Christmas, Morgan," he says, placing a soft kiss on the corner of my mouth. "Thank you for inviting me to be here when Liam wakes up."

I smile and place my hand on his chest. "I'm glad you're here. This is the best Christmas I've had in a long time." I motion for him to move into the living room. "Make yourself comfortable. I'll start a pot of coffee."

"Actually..." Brant pauses. "I left some things in my truck; I'll go out and grab them while you're doing that."

Curious about what he is going to get, I narrow my eyes and smile. "What have you been up to?" I ask, my heart fluttering. Since we came to an understanding the day we visited William's grave, things have been more wonderful than I could've ever hoped for.

Brant has been here, checking the water in the tree, sweeping up pine needles, and anything else I've needed. Often before I've realized something needs doing. He even took time off to come see Liam play the role of a sheep in his class Christmas play.

"It's a surprise," he says, smiling widely. "You'll have to wait and see."

Deciding he isn't going to change his mind and tell me, I head to the kitchen and start that pot of coffee. I lean on the counter and wait for the gurgling to start, indicating the precious liquid will be ready soon. I can't believe how much my life has changed in a few short months.

The door quietly swishes open, and clicks shut again, before the rustling of bags captures my attention, pulling me from my place at the counter. I turn the corner into the living room in time to see Brant bent down placing boxes and bags under the tree. The few gifts that were there are now mixed in with several others that are bigger and more brightly decorated.

"Brant!" I gasp. "That is way too much!"

Brant looks over his shoulder from his place by the tree. "It's never too much when it comes from the heart," he says.

A lightness fills my belly, and a tear breaks free, sliding down my cheeks. "Brant," I whisper. "I don't need gifts to know you care, and neither does Liam." The tender way he has cared for us these past few months shows us the depth of his affection far more than a gift ever could. "Your presence is our present."

Brant stands and walks to me, wrapping me in his arms. "Morgan, I know you don't care about the presents, but I do. I want to spend the rest of my life showing you how much you are treasured."

Pulling back, he reaches into his pocket and pulls out a soft velvet pouch. "I can't wait to give you this."

I gasp. "Brant, what did you do?" He hands me the small satchel and I try to get it open. "My hands are shaking too badly; will you open it?" I ask, handing it back.

Brant smiles and opens the pouch and empties it onto my open palm. A gold ring with a beautiful diamond-encrusted knot in the middle sparkles in the early morning light. Tears burn the corners of my eyes. "Brant..."

"It's a promise ring," he says, tipping my face to look at him. "I know you're not ready for me to propose, but I want you to know I'm not going anywhere."

Brant takes the ring and slides it onto the ring finger of my right hand.

"Brant, it's beautiful! I don't know what to say. You didn't have to do this." I can't stop looking at the ring now on my finger. A promise ring. I look up at Brant, his smile lights up the room.

"You deserve to be spoiled sometimes too." He leans in and kisses me softly. The gentle feel of his lips on mine thaws the last bit of my fear away. He is here to stay.

"Mommy," Liam calls from the hallway. "Did Santa come?" His sleepy little face turns the corner and sees Brant and me standing with our arms wrapped around one another. "Yes!" he shouts. "My secret wish came true!"

Confused, I look at Brant to see if he knows what Liam is talking about. Shrugging, he smiles. "What secret wish?"

"I asked Santa if you could marry my mommy and be my new daddy! And it worked—you're here!" Liam rushes over, throwing his arms around us. "I wonder if I got the racetrack, too!" he shouts, racing to the tree.

"Wow," he whispers, eyes as big as saucers. "Look at all these presents! Can we open them now, please, Mommy?"

"Of course," I say smiling. Taking Brant's hand in mine, we settle into the sofa side by side, coffee momentarily forgotten in Liam's enthusiasm.

"Here, Mommy," he says, handing me a flat box wrapped in gold paper. "This one's for you."

Carefully, I tear back the paper, and lift the lid off the box. Nestled inside green tissue paper is the plate I had looked at during the tree lighting ceremony at the end of November. "How in the world?" I ask, gingerly lifting the plate from its protective home. "I didn't even know you saw me looking at this. When did you have time to buy it? We were together the whole day!" Hot tears of joy wet my face.

Brant shifts on the couch. "Well, not the whole day. I used the restroom, remember?" A hint of red stains his cheeks. "I saw you looking at it, and wanted to get it for you, so I made a little detour while you were busy with Liam."

"Thank you," I say, holding the plate to my chest. "This is perfect."

Liam wiggles on the floor, clearly done waiting for his turn. "Can I go next?" he asks, pointing to the largest of the presents under the tree.

"Go ahead," I say, laughing as he pulls the big box into the center of the rug and tears the race car paper off with enthusiasm.

"A racetrack!" he yells, jumping up from his spot on the floor and dancing in a circle. "He did it! He really did it!" Liam grabs the box and runs over to the couch. "Can we open it now, Mommy? I want to race cars with Brant."

Laughing, I hand Brant the box. "Why don't you open the rest of your presents first, and then you can play while I make breakfast?"

Liam nods, and dashes back to the tree. After opening the slime, and the game I'd placed under the tree, Liam opens the other remaining bags and boxes revealing a new sweater with Brant's Automotive written on the front, a kid-size tool set, and a new set of fireman pajamas.

The rest of the day passes in a blur of building racetracks, racing cars, and playing games with Liam. Brant hasn't stopped smiling, and neither have I.

Liam is at the table playing with his slime, and Brant and I are cuddled onto the sofa enjoying the temporary calm. "I love you," I say leaning further into his side.

He squeezes me a little tighter. "I love you too, Morgan," he whispers, kissing the top of my head.

Best. Christmas. *Ever.*

If you enjoyed Morgan and Brant's story, I'd love it if you would consider leaving a review on Amazon, Goodreads, or BookBub! It always brings a smile to my face when I read a new review!

Can't get enough of the friendship between the characters in Piney Brook? Keep reading for a sneak peak at Daniel and Reese's story. Sweet Summertime Wishes available now on Amazon and included in Kindle Unlimited. https://tinyurl.com/SweetSummertimeWishes

Want to know how Brant pops the question? Sign up for my newsletter and get access to a special bonus scene. https://tinyurl.com/HisChristmasWishBonusEpilogue

About Author

Tia Marlee resides in Central Texas with her husband and three teenaged children. When she isn't writing, Tia enjoys reading, embroidery and spending time with her family. Tia is the author of the Piney Brook Wishes series featuring unexpected love stories based in small-town Piney Brook, Arkansas. She has also written for the multi-author Coffee Loft Series.

Also By Tia Marlee

Piney Brook Wishes Series
His Christmas Wish
Sweet Summertime Wishes
Wishing for the Girl Next Door
A Soldier's Wish

The Coffee Loft Series
Bean Wishing for a Latte Love
You Mocha Me Crazy

Let's Stay In Touch

You can find me at my website: https://tiamarlee.com
Follow me:
Facebook: https://tinyurl.com/FBTiaMarlee
Instagram: https://tinyurl.com/IGTiaMarlee
Amazon: https://tinyurl.com/AmazonTiaMarlee
BookBub: https://tinyurl.com/BBTiaMarlee
Goodreads: https://tinyurl.com/GRTiaMarlee

Join my reader group: https://tinyurl.com/TiaMarleeReaderGroup

Acknowledgments

This book wouldn't be possible without the love and support of my amazing husband and children. I'm grateful every day for your encouragement to pursue my dreams.

To my author friends who have supported me every step of the way, thank you. Your guidance and willingness to answer so many questions has been life altering.

It's always been my dream to write a book. Thank you to all the readers who have decided to take a chance on a new author. You'll forever have a place in my heart.

Printed in Great Britain
by Amazon